TENTACLES OF TERROR

Bruce Herbert Scott

TENTACLES OF TERROR

Fiction4All

Chapter 1 – Falling from the Sky

It was not the three loud bangs in quick succession coming from the rear of the aircraft that worried me; it was the look of sheer terror on the face of the flight attendant.

The aircraft began to convulse in a vigorous shudder and the inevitability of a crash landing dawned upon me. It was an old Boeing 737 owned by FastAir a private airline that contracts to large mining and oil exploration companies in Indonesia. They transport staff to remote mines and oil fields throughout the archipelago. This time this old girl wasn't going to make it.

I was sitting beside the port over wing emergency exit. This wasn't an accident. Quite apart from the safety aspect, I always try to get allocated this seat since the bit of extra space that is often given to these seats is more comfortable for a tall guy like me to sit in. Mind you, from the way this old bird was shaking and slipping around in the sky I wondered if my seat position would make any difference at all. Strangely, I wasn't afraid, but I was suddenly thrown into a challenge to survive and I began to rapidly take steps to tip the odds in my favor.

Since my eardrums had not blown out and the oxygen masks had not been released, I guessed that the integrity of the cabin was still holding up, at least for now. The plane was yawing drunkenly from left to right and the angle of incidence was rapidly changing from a climbing attitude to a dive. Obviously, the pilot was having very great difficulty controlling the aircraft but at least that was more encouraging than if we were in an uncontrolled spin or a dive. The flight attendant disappeared from my view as she ran to an empty seat and presumably strapped herself in.

I had long ago decided that the "brace position" described in the safety announcements was nonsense and so I proceeded to wedge myself into my seat by bringing my feet up and pushing hard on the seat in front. I also busied myself by wrapping the airline supplied blanket about my head and upper body. I wedged the edges around my glasses leaving the tiniest gap to look through to minimize exposure to the fire that must inevitably result. With my now restricted vision I concentrated on the emergency hatch and rehearsed the action of releasing the hatch ensuring that I could find the handle and open it in the dark. I put the small airline pillow between the seat belt and my belly and pulled the belt up as tightly as I could bear.

The attractive Asian woman sitting beside me obviously thought that I had the right idea. I became aware of her watching what I was doing and was following my actions. I noticed for the first time that she was also wearing Levis like I was and I hoped that the thick denim might offer us some small protection in the likely event of there being flames after the crash. I was wearing a leather coat not because I was cold but so that I could keep my papers and money secure in the inner pockets rather than in the more vulnerable pockets of my jeans. I had noticed when she first sat down that she was wearing a tight fitting woolen top that displayed the very pleasing shape of her body. Possibly, I might have been a bit too obvious in noticing this and she had not spoken to me since sitting down.

Somewhere deep in my brain was the realization that I wanted her to survive if I did.

The screams of the other passengers filled the aircraft as the ground loomed closer. The oxygen masks had still not been released and if the cabin crew was doing anything I certainly wasn't aware of it.

The impact was every bit as bad as I expected and the noise of shattering metal was overwhelming. I still have no idea what took place other than the fact that the plane hit the ground in a shallow dive and proceeded to disintegrate. The forces acting on my body were so violent and various that I fully expected my body to breakup just as the aircraft was doing. After what seemed like an eternity we came to a violent stop. Despite being upside down at one point in the hurly burly of the crash, we were right way up when our section of the fuselage came to rest. Forcing my bruised muscles to move, I followed the drill that I had been rehearsing on the way down and very quickly opened the hatch. A silent prayer of gratitude flashed through my brain as the hatch came away cleanly and it had not frozen in place from the mechanical stresses placed on the aircraft. Somebody at Boeing had certainly got it right.

I heard the girl undo her seat belt and I grabbed her and pulled her over my lap and threw her bodily out through the hole. I jumped out after her and we slid across the stub of the wing that still remained attached to the aircraft and our feet touched the ground. Actually, it was mud, as we were in a rice paddy. I could see smoke on the opposite side of the aircraft and fire in some nearby debris, an engine, as I later worked out. The smell of fuel permeated the air. We ran!

If you can call sloshing through the mud running as fast as one can then I guess that is what we did. We were some one hundred feet from the fuselage when the first explosion occurred and the blast of superheated air hit us in the back and knocked us face down into the mud. This was not such a bad place to be as there was protection in the cool mud and the air was cooler near the ground. Moreover, a couple of inches of cool water covered the mud and this was helpful as well. We learnt very quickly to submerge ourselves in the cool muck and escape the heat and fumes swirling above. Each breath was a gamble as to whether we would breathe cool air or a blast of heat and acrid fumes. Fortunately, as the fire took hold of the aircraft, the airflow began to stabilize into cool air being drawn in close to the ground to feed the fire while the very hot air rose vertically above the burning aircraft. In any event, it became possible for us to crawl, swim and slither through the mud assisted by pulling on handfuls of immature rice plants as we distanced ourselves from the fire.

We made our way across the paddy and fell into an irrigation canal filled with water that even to my heat seared nostrils still smelt foul. The depth ranged from knee deep to shoulder depth and we waded and swam upstream away from the blazing aircraft wreckage. The canal was fed from a pipe approximately one metre in diameter. I was looking for a way out of the canal as the girl took my wrist firmly and pulled me into the pipe. We sat pushed close together, gasping for breath, as a small trickle of clean water dammed behind our bodies and swirled around us and began to wash the foul accumulation of mud and slime from our legs.

"We hide here," she said. It was the first time that I had heard her speak since she boarded the plane. Her voice was hoarse from breathing the smoke and fire and the effort of speaking made her cough. In a croaking whisper and speaking in Bahasa Indonesia I said, "Why hide?" Replying in Bahasa that was obviously her first language she said, "just hide". She closed her eyes and put her head on my shoulder and made it clear that she did not want to speak any more. I can't say that I felt much like talking at that point either. I became aware of the burning in my throat and the riot of pains surging from every part of my body. I was unable to distinguish which pain was from which of the bruises or torn ligaments, there were so many.

We had sat huddled together for some thirty minutes catching our breath and unwinding from the exertion. I was wondering why she saw a need for us to hide until I heard a military aircraft approaching from over the sea. It turned out to be an A-4e Skyhawk. The pilot came in very low and with the nose high in order to fly as slowly as possible. Clearly, he was examining the wreck as best he could from the air. It was clear to us that we were the only survivors but he wouldn't have seen any sign of life. There were a couple of blackened shapes near the exit from which we escaped but it was impossible to tell if they were bodies or what they were. In any event, we were in no frame of mind to go back even if we were up to it. There was no evidence of our escape as the water had covered our path through the paddy and by walking up the canal there was no evidence of our progress up there either. I stood and began to move to the entrance of the pipe in an effort to attract the attention of the pilot. The girl grabbed my shoulders and pushed me down. She shook her head vigorously and told me to stay where I was and to say nothing.

After a couple of passes over the site the aircraft flew away and stillness descended over the area.

"I think we should talk" I croaked.

She nodded and obviously feeling that she had more to explain than I did, she began to tell her story in a painful whisper.

Chapter 2 – Leni's Betrayal

She began by very formally introducing herself as Leni Hong. She is an Indonesian citizen of Chinese descent whose family, like many others, had lived in Jakarta for many generations. Her parents owned two stores where they sold computer software and hardware. One store had been in the Glodok shopping area and it had been looted and burnt out in the riots of 1998 when the Suharto presidency came to an end. Her mother who had been working in the store when the rioting began was fortunate to escape without being raped and killed. This happened to many others at that time. Their other store is in the Munga Dua center and is still operating. Leni went to the University of Jakarta where she studied Information Technology.

Since leaving University, four years ago, she worked for the defense forces as a civilian contractor and became a network administrator at the army headquarters in Jakarta. She said that she was very good at what she did and despite some personal bias against her, she had achieved respect as a professional.

She didn't need to explain that as a female non-Javanese catholic there would have been few to assist her in achieving a career in the Moslem dominated armed forces.

One of her duties as network administrator was to check any emails that had been rejected by the network firewall.

Her difficulties had begun when she opened an email which had been incorrectly addressed and had been routed to her support desk. The email was from a senior officer, Brigadier General Ismail Purnomo, who had been temporally stationed in Timor Timur (East Timor) where he had been posted in order to suppress the breakaway movement there. The address of the email had been sent (with one character missing from the correct email address) to lieutenant General Ibraham Setepu in the Jakarta headquarters.

Setepu as a two-star general would never have spoken to a lowly IT contractor, much less a Chinese female, but she had seen him from time to time in the building.

She had been told that her job as a network administrator not only involved the technical security of the military system but that it was everyone's duty to report on any activity that might subvert the government. As she read the email, she was aghast at the contents of the message. She was shocked but not surprised that such a sensitive message had been sent by email as many older officers in the defense forces did not really understand the security risks in email traffic, while they were only too aware of the obvious uncertainty of most other communications mediums in Indonesia.

The email congratulated Setepu on the role that he had played in securing the election of Bacharuddin Jusuf Habibie as the National President and expressed his delight in seeing such a qualified and successful engineer in the position with a strong sense of altruism but a weak sense of political judgement. He stated that Habibie was too soft on protesters and was certainly not the friend of the military that former president Suharto had been. He stated that the alliance between the military and the ruling Golkar party in frustrating the appointment of Megawati Sukarnoputri of the PDI permangan party despite its electoral majority was a great success. Purnomo advocated that an even stronger stance should be taken by the military in suppressing student protestors and that some needed be shot as a warning to the others to cease causing the disruption.

Purnomo referred to the alliance between Setepu and retired General Makarim who was now a sitting member of the MPR (the national parliament) and remarked on how wonderful it would be if Makarim could get elected president and appoint Setepu as commander of the Kopassus

In a western country, it would have been inappropriate for senior officers in the defense forces to discuss political matters in private much less in official channels; however, in Indonesia, this was the sort of discussion that occurred daily between Moslem officers across the nation. It was what came next that really shocked her.

The email also referred to an earlier discussion that they had and, as requested, he had arranged for his contacts in the Armed Forces Intelligence Agency (Kopassus), to investigate all the elected members of the MPR.

Attached was a lengthy document in which the names of all the elected members had been listed. The political allegiances of each one was identified and whether or not they were considered hostile to Makarim being elected. If the individual was loyal to Habibie then he had listed out how each these members could through blackmail or intimidation be made to vote for Makarim.

He had also investigated all military officers above the rank of captain and had supplied the names and locations of those who could be expected to support Makarim if a majority vote could not be ensured and that a military overthrow of the Government was required.

The list made interesting reading, some members had a history of being bought off on past occasions while others had shown that they would vote according to who they could be convinced would win. Some of the clearly hostile members had weakness for women, drugs or cash but most were shown to respond best to coercion by more direct methods. The names of lovers and close family members were also printed against each name.

Leni was trapped. If she deleted the message, then sooner or later Purnomo would find out that Setepu did not get the message and in view of the sensitive nature of the message. He would then use his many contacts to find out where it went and identify that she was on duty at the time. On the other hand, if she corrected the address and passed it on she was caught again because they would know that she had seen it.

Her supervisor was the IT Manager. Rudi Ryadi had supported her in her career and had recommended her for the position that she held. Not only was he her boss but she felt that he was a friend also. She printed the message and showed it to him. Rudi was very supportive and told her to tear up the message and that he would record a network crash in the log and delete any record of the message ever having been received or processed. Should anyone contact the IT group the system crash would be noted and whoever took the call would explain that no message was received. Leni thanked Rudi and went back to her workstation.

She trusted Rudi but on an impulse (feminine intuition perhaps?) she created a new email user id and used this to copy the message to a server, called XDRIVE, on the internet where, for a small annual fee, one can save data securely. Then she deleted the user id and all record of the copy was removed.

She tried to work for about an hour with the events whirling in her mind. So much hung on her boss keeping his word and protecting her from the situation into which she had so innocently been drawn. She busied herself checking system backup logs and other boring tasks to take her mind off the situation. Then the phone rang. It was Anita the other network administrator. Anita told her that the Military Police and Kopassus officers had visited her and had, with much intimidation, tried to get her to say that Leni was a subversive and was behind anti Muslim protests. Anita, though a Muslim lady, was one of the great many Indonesians who despised religious bigotry and had been a good friend to Leni since she had started work at defense headquarters. Knowing that Anita had risked her life in phoning her she thanked her most gratefully and said that one day she hoped that they would meet again.

Leni knew that she had to flee immediately.

Tearfully she rung her mother and briefly told her what had happened then tried to leave the building. She found her security swipe card would no longer open the door of the server room. She told one of the operators that she had left her card at home and that she was going home to get it. She borrowed the friendly operator's card and went outside. Then she passed the card back to the operator through the window of the lady's toilet as had long been the practice of female staff who didn't want to get into trouble for absent mindedness. She had never done it before but knew that the operators did it often.

She ran to her car and waved to the guard at the gate as she drove out. Fortunately, the gate only needed a swipe card to enter but opened automatically to allow cars to leave. She drove to the Plaza Indonesia and left her Mazda in the busy car park knowing that she would never see it again. Thoughtfully she took all personal papers from the glove compartment. The police might find it eventually but it would take some time before anybody reported it as abandoned. More than likely somebody would steal it if it was left overnight.

Avoiding security cameras where she could, and walking sideways and window shopping avidly, Leni made her way to a Muslim clothing store. She bought a jilbab and matching hijab. She chose a bright violet and white pattern in the style that Islamic women of her age wore to the office. She got changed in the store telling the assistant that she was going to visit her mother. "Inshall allah" (God is great) she smiled as she walked out of the store. Figuring that the security forces would be looking for a girl in western clothing, the Islamic clothing would possibly assist in diverting attention while the veil would hide her face to some extent. For the only time in her life she wished that she lived in Afghanistan or one of the other Arab countries where the veil covers the entire face. Indonesian Muslim women usually show their face. This is to be consistent with the story of the discussion with Mohammed in which he was supposedly asked what parts of the body Muslim women should show to the world. He pointed to his hands and face. Indonesian Muslims like to joke that the reasons that the Arab women cover their entire face is because the flies are so bad over there.

She wore the veil well forward and with her face down in the subservient attitude adopted by many Indonesian Muslim women. She was virtually unrecognizable as the confident young westernized woman who had earlier entered the building. Her next visit was to the banks where she took as much cash as possible from her Bank Lippo account and also from the special savings account that she ran at the Negara Bank. She was fearful that her accounts may already have been frozen and that she would attract attention, and possibly even taken into custody, at the bank. She waited with her heart pounding and watching the tellers on both occasions. She was trying to look relaxed as despite the sensitivity she had for any unusual behavior. She almost panicked as the Bank Lippo teller went away and consulted somebody else. Fighting the impulse to run, she waited for his return and relaxed when she returned to the counter and asked for additional identification in view of the large amount that she was withdrawing.

Her legs felt like jelly as she left the bank and went to a jewelry store where she bought necklaces and bracelets worth about ten million Rupiah and charged them to her credit cards. She also bought an ostentatious but cheap camera and put it in a shopping bag. Although her spending amounted to only about one thousand two hundred US Dollars, she had spent more money in one day than she had managed to save in the past year. She sat near some teenagers on a bench in the shopping center and placed her mobile phone beside her. Feigning absent mindedness, she walked off and left it on the seat. As expected one of them stole the phone and ran away. She hoped that he and his friends would make lots of calls as they traveled around so that the police in monitoring the calls (as they can easily and frequently do) would look for her in those areas. Since the phone was supplied to her by the defense force she had little to fear from getting a huge bill not that she expected to be available or alive to pay it anyway.

She then caught a taxi and drove north to the port of Ancol (pronounced Anchol) where she had a meal in a restaurant beside the water. She sat and watched the children trying various methods to tug at the hearts of visiting tourists and the pimps endeavoring to solicit business from any male that they could find. Even with a nose that had grown up in Jakarta with its stinking canals of stagnant water, a design disaster which was a legacy of Dutch occupation, her dinner was spoilt by the smell of the putrid water flowing around the dock. Ancol is the final exit point of the Jakarta canal system to the sea.

Paying cash, she bought a ticket and paid for three night's accommodation at the island resort of Pulau Putri. This delightful island is one of the Pulau Seribu (thousand island) group and Pulau Putri (daughter island) offers the best value for money. It caters for the few overseas tourists who still visited Jakarta, and on her Indonesian salary it was still expensive. However, she knew from previous experience that the staff do not ask to see an ID card and so she hoped to buy a few nights of quiet while she decided what next to do.

Finding a toilet, she removed the jilbab and hijab and stashed then into her bag. Then, with the camera slung around her neck, she began to behave as a tourist until the boat arrived. The usual crush of prospective guides began to hound her to show off the sights of the port. At the earliest opportunity, she boarded the ferry with its four powerful outboards. The high-speed dash over the surging sea with the salty spray splashing through the window offered some diversion from her desperate situation.

She couldn't relax during her three days on the island. Beautiful as the surroundings and the food were, they could not distract her from replaying the events in her mind repeatedly. The traitorous behavior of two respected generals and the danger that she now faced worried her of course - but it was the treachery of Ryadi whom she had previously thought of as a friend that keep stealing into her mind every time that she relaxed. She found herself lying wide awake well before sunrise going over conversations she had had with him and conversations that she would like to have had. Whenever she made a conscious effort to put the thoughts from her mind, the respite lasted only briefly before she found herself dwelling on the issues again.

Using an internet café at the resort, she emailed her paternal cousin, Joyce, who was a very good friend as the two girls had gone through university together. She had had no reason to mention Joyce to her employer and felt that not only would it be safe to contact her, but Joyce was married to Hendrick, a young businessman who had been recently elected to the DPR at the last election as a PDI member. Joyce arranged to meet her at Dunkin Donuts, a small franchise in an office block in the main street of the city the following day.

Leni was embarrassed at having to involve her cousin in her plight, as she felt guilty at not having seen her very often since she had got her job at the Defense Headquarters. She was sure that Joyce would do all that she could to assist her not only because of strong family loyalties but because she was a good friend. Moreover, Joyce was every bit as committed to democratic processes as was Leni. Though a good student, the attractive and vivacious Joyce, had known, from the moment that she had met Hendrick, that she wanted nothing more than to be his wife and the mother to his children. Hendrick, was a tall and very serious young man of high status Javanese ancestry. He was not one for small talk and though his identity card identified him as a Moslem, he had never been to a mosque since he was a child. He had studied a business degree at the University of Jakarta. His family had not been happy at his marrying a Chinese girl but, despite this, on graduation had been absorbed into his grandfather's transport business. Through his achievements, he soon won the respect of the older family members. On the retirement of his grandfather, he took control of the company. Hendrick was devoted to his wife and the couple doted on their daughter born three months ago.

To maintain her tourist facade, Leni caught one of the more luxurious Golden Bird taxis after she alighted from the ferry on her return to Ancol. Speaking in English and trying to do so with an American accent she told the driver where she wished to go. Sitting back in the air-conditioned Nissan Cedric; she relaxed and wondered what she could do next. She had hoped to arrive inconspicuously at the office block however the 'helpful' driver after waving to the security guard at the gate drove almost in the door of the restaurant causing office workers to scatter in their path. She paid the driver 60,000 Rupiah and returned his beaming smile.

Avoiding the glares from the office workers she made her way inside to where Joyce, breast feeding baby Amber Hendrick Putri, was waiting for her. Leni's eyes filled with tears on seeing a friendly face but it was the realization that, by her presence, she was placing this mother and baby in mortal danger that made her sob

18

uncontrollably. The two young women hugged each other and sat down. Leni said, "I can't do this – it's too much to ask of you" she kissed her cousin and began to leave. Joyce pressed her hand down on her cousin's thigh saying, "if they find you then we will all be in trouble." In her anxious and emotional state Leni accepted this dubious assertion and allowed Joyce to dominate the meeting enjoying the simple luxury of being cared for. On finishing their coffee and over sweet donuts (especially to Indonesian tastes) the girls got to their feet and Joyce while shielding baby Amber's eyes from the bright sunlight, led Leni to her Mercedes parked nearby.

On seeing his charges walking to the car, Ujang the driver ran over from the shade where he had been waiting beside the building. He took the baby from her mother and strapped her into her capsule with practiced efficiency. He then ran around to open the other back door for the two cousins to enter. Ujang greeted Leni affectionately and with great respect but showed no surprise on seeing her. Leni surmised that Joyce had told him that she would be meeting her and had no doubt told him to be discrete. Ujang had been assigned as Hendrick's driver and bodyguard when he had first joined his grandfather's company some years before. Now that Hendrick and Joyce were married, Ujang had been given the task of driving and being bodyguard for Joyce. This giant of a man, with teeth that were an orthodontic disaster in a face that bore evidence of countless fights while growing up in the back streets of Jakarta, doted on the young mother and daughter like they were his own – which in a sense, they were.

Relaxing in the car and with the reassuring presence of Ujang, Joyce became more like the cousin Leni had grown up with. She was a very demonstrative person with hands that never stayed still as she spoke. She was tactile as well. She would frequently touch her cousin's leg and hands unconsciously as she talked enthusiastically about what a great man Hendrick is and like any new mother, she talked about Amber as if she was the only baby in the world.

That evening over a dinner of Babi (Pork) Sate with katjang (peanut) sauce and Bami Goring (fried egg noodles) washed down with coke (very few Indonesians drink alcohol) Leni told her entire story to Hendrick. She broke down and cried at various points during her tale especially in describing Rudi's treachery and when she described her phone call to her mother. Hendrick sat impassively and listened intently as she spoke. Joyce hugged her cousin and frequently gave reassuring smiles as she listened to her story. All the while, Amber suckled contentedly on her mother's breast.

On finishing her tale, Hendrick nodded knowingly and called for Ujang and recounted the main elements of her story to him. Leni felt uncomfortable having Ujang being brought into the picture but she trusted Hendrick and realized that she had no choice but to trust his judgment. The fact that Joyce was obviously very relaxed in Ujang's presence made her comfortable.

"Are you sure that you weren't followed?" Hendrick asked Leni, but it was Ujang who answered with a shake of his head and a look that said, "nobody follows me".

With the air of authority often assumed by Indonesian men when talking to women, Hendrick said to Joyce "Look after her and keep her out of sight." To Ujang he said, "Come with me – we have some work to do".

Chapter 3 - Leni Finds a Sanctuary

The two women stayed indoors for the remainder of the day, Leni reveling in being able to assist Joyce in looking after Amber. She bathed the wriggling baby with Joyce giving instructions. Like all non-mothers, she was surprised at the difficulty of the task and terrified that the soapy little body would slip from her grasp or have her little face go under the water. Amber like any baby could sense Leni's anxiety and cried and wriggled with all the energy of her healthy little body.

Eventually, bathed and powdered with a fresh nappy and in her little pink jumpsuit the baby girl latched on to her mother's proffered nipple and suckled happily.

The time she spent with Joyce as she recounted the story of Amber's birth and her life with Hendrick drew Leni's mind away from the terrors of the last few days. Amber's birth was perfectly normal and routine by medical standards but obviously not to Joyce. Leni enjoyed the intimacy that only two close females could enjoy as Joyce recounted the details of the birth in virtually a contraction by contraction story with all the pains and bodily functions graphically described.

Two breasts later Joyce put the now contentedly sleeping baby in her cot. She needed to be careful not to wake her up by bumping any of the plethora of brightly colored toys hanging from above the cot. They were positioned in expectation of the day in the near future when the little child would have the dexterity to catch them.

While Amber slept contentedly, Joyce used the few hours of freedom to fuss around the house. Even though she had a housemaid she enjoyed keeping things just right especially when it came to folding Amber's freshly washed clothes and putting them away.

Leni made herself useful by using her considerable skills to update the operating system of Joyce's computer and setting up a separate email account that Joyce could use by herself without needing to share Hendrick's account. It was not that there were any problems between them but it was more convenient if she didn't need to trawl through Hendrick's business correspondence looking for her messages. More importantly, Hendrick would no longer need to wait while baby pictures uploaded and downloaded to Joyce's friends.

Joyce was cooking dinner when Hendrick walked in followed by Ujang.

Despite the reciprocal warmth between the family and Ujang, it would have been culturally inappropriate for him to sit and have dinner with the family. Instead, Joyce interrupted the dinner preparation (and in doing so caused the rice to become gluggy) and the two women sat and listened to what the two men had to report.

Hendrick had spent the afternoon in his office and had confirmed from his contacts that no official alert had been issued by the Defense Department for Leni but that confidential messages had indeed been sent through branches of government in which militant Islamist thinking prevailed. In these messages, there was indeed an alert for Leni and her description had been circulated to these partisan security services and police.

Leni was shocked not only by her being the subject of such alerts but by the existence of this subversive communications network.

"But, how did you find this out?" she asked.

The two men looked at her impassively and behaved as if they hadn't heard her question.

"Don't ask!" her cousin whispered, "You don't need to know."

Ujang, she was told, had driven to Munga Dua and visited Gladys Hong's (Leni's mother's) store and purchased a computer hard drive. He had studied the various bits of computer hardware in the store without even the faintest idea of what any of them did. He judged his moment to go to the counter when the woman who wore a name tag with "Gladys" on it was free. Pointing under the glass counter to a mysterious square object with a slot in front he asked for the "Seagate" which was the largest word printed on the label along with other incomprehensible information. As he handed the bundle of Rupiah notes to the anxious woman he passed a note with the words "dia aman" (she is safe) written on it.

Placing the item in a bag and giving him much more change than she needed to, the anxious mother stared deeply into his eyes and said "Terima Kasih" (thank you) with much more emphasis than would have been appropriate for a mere hardware purchase. Engaging his attention, she then pointedly gazed across the aisle to the shop opposite which specialized in selling bootleg software and videos.

Ujang then went to the software shop and started looking through the racks of videos with their photocopied labels. He subtly watched another man in the store who had been there from before he first went in to Bu (Mrs) Hong's store. He was flicking aimlessly through the racks. Taking his time, Ujang carefully selected the Nicole Kidman and Tom Cruise movie "Eyes Wide Shut" and left the store leaving the "shopper" who by this time had been through every rack and was starting to go around again. Not surprisingly he seemed to show greatest interest in those racks of goods giving the clearest view of Bu Hong's store.

Ujang left and watched carefully to see if he was being followed. After browsing through other stores, he had a leisurely pizza at the Pizza Hut and now quite confident that he was alone made his way to the car walking past the bootleg software and the "shopper" who was still looking through the racks. He then drove back to Hendrick's office to pick him up and take him home.

Hendrick then picked up the conversation and told Leni that he had booked her on a flight on an aircraft owned by a charter company which was flying some mining employees and contractors to Lombok who were then going to get a helicopter to Nusa Tengara mine. As it turned out, Laurie was one of those contractors.

He had booked her into a cheap hotel in Lombok where she was to pretend to be a novelist and stay there until he could work out what to do next.

The flight was due to leave in two weeks' time and Leni was to stay out of sight at their house during that time.

After a blissful two weeks during which time little Amber got to recognize "Aunty Leni" and Leni, in turn, showered her affection on her little niece it was time to go.

Joyce went shopping and bought Leni suitable travel wear including a couple of Moslem veils. Hendrick gave her a money belt for her to wear under her clothing and one of Joyce's nursing bras in which the large cups had been thickly lined with 100,000 Rupiah notes.

She had no idea how much money she wore about her body and was uncomfortable with the money belt and the ill-fitting bra. Moreover, she was deeply self-conscious of her enhanced bust size.

No wonder she was embarrassed when she caught Laurie looking at her as we boarded the plane.

Chapter 4 – Laurie Takes Stock

There we were, sitting in a pipe, muddy, bruised and with nothing but the clothes that we wore. Leni was convinced that our aircraft had been shot down because she figured that somehow, they must have known that she was aboard. Knowing the attitude of many in the TNI and the Kopassus at that time I felt that whilst one could not be certain that she was right; it would have been unwise to ignore her caution.

We were both badly bruised where the seat belt had held us down and my back ached from whatever it was that had happened to it as I had been tossed around. Leni was similarly bruised and her right elbow was very sore from where she had bashed it on the armrest.

We discussed our injuries and agreed that we had done remarkably well considering what we had been through. She cried as we talked about the many passengers and crew who were not nearly so lucky and I must admit that I nearly did the same.

Fortunately, the clothes that we wore had certain advantages. Apart from the money that Leni carried about her body, I was still carrying my Australian passport as well as the South African one that I had been issued with whilst I was working there. I also had two wallets. I had read in an Australian Special Air Services book some years ago, recommending that one should carry a decoy wallet in an obvious location and one's real wallet in a more hidden location. Based on this advice, I always carried a decoy wallet in my hip pocket and a second real wallet tucked into an inner pocket of my coat. The decoy had about 60,000 Rupiah ($10) in it and a few out of date credit cards. The idea was that if I was ever attacked I would quickly drop the decoy on the ground and run. Likewise, a pickpocket would see the clear outline of the decoy and go for that. It was an idea that made good sense. Particularly in some of the unsavory neighborhoods that I found myself in as I travelled around. I had about 100,000,000 Rupiah and about $5000 Australian dollars in my real wallet.

I have never been attacked but the decoy wallet did disappear one day as I was shopping in Pasa Raya in Jakarta. Since I am considerably taller than most Indonesians they would probably go after softer targets than try to physically attack me.

Also, in my coat, I carry a mace sprayer. It is difficult to carry a gun when you travel and even though I am licensed to carry one it draws attention to me when checking it in and out at airports. I considered carrying a knife but with a knife one needs to get close to one's attacker and you can only disable one at a time. The mace sprayer enables you to reduce your attackers to a bunch of crybabies while you can suitably dispatch your targets with your bare hands. I bought the sprayer from a shop called "Dads Toys" in Cape Town many years ago. It doesn't draw attention and looks like a very masculine after shave dispenser but God help anyone who accidently sprayed himself with it.

There are also fewer problems if an attacker was to run away from you with burning eyes and a runny nose rather than if he was left lying on the footpath with holes in him.

Leni had begun speaking to me in English which was every bit as good as the Bahasa Indonesia that I had learnt from my many years travelling in Indonesia and Malaya. We had a bit of much needed lightness when she was describing her bruises but pronounced them as "bruces" as most Indonesian people struggle with that unfamiliar sound. Who is Bruce? I asked and I heard her laugh for the first time – I'd never seen a pretty face light up as much as Leni's did when she smiled.

She asked me about my life and since she had been so open with me I started to tell my story – maybe I could make her laugh again.

Chapter 5 - Laurie's Story

I was born and grew up in Brisbane Australia. My father Gordon Hudson was a great man who made quite a lot of money after he started building what Australians call caravans and what the Americans call trailers. My mother was a very beautiful blonde woman who had been a TV hostess in a quiz show before becoming a very loving full-time mother. They named me, Laurie. In high school, my mates started calling me "Truck"; a nickname that was to follow me for the rest of my life.

As a kid, I always wanted to be a police officer even though I was very good at mathematics computing and science. I certainly met the height and fitness requirements and despite my parents wanting me to continue my education by going to university, I joined the Queensland police service when I had finished high school.

I started at the bottom and worked my way through the system. I had walked the beat. I had been kicked and vomited on by drunks. I had fought off crazy druggies when I busted them and went to seize their stash and I even worked under cover for many months while I was working with the drug squad.

It was during my time in the police that I met Angela. She was a forensic scientist who was employed by the Queensland Health Department but she was contracted to the police service. I guess we originally hit it off because of my interest in computing and science. I learnt a lot from her. Eventually our relationship became more physical than professional. We were married 2 years after we first met.

I was lucky the way it happened because the way I dressed (and smelt) during the times that I was working under cover, I doubt if I would ever have met a decent woman with whom I could have developed a relationship. Not that I didn't get frequent offers from drug crazed harpies who looked and smelt worse than I did.

Some months after we were married (less than nine) our son Regan was born.

After maternity leave, Angela went back to working part time. I started applying to get out of the drug squad and applied to join the newly formed Technology Crime Unit. I didn't want to have to leave Regan for weeks on end while I lived with my targets nor did I want him to have a dad who looked like a drop out.

It was a happy 5 years watching Regan grow and Angela and I grew more devoted to each other. We kept trying to create a brother or sister for Regan but no luck.

One day I was walking to the shop with Regan who had our Labrador dog on a leash, Regan had named it Bert – even though she was female. Bert saw another dog on the other side of the road and ran across the road to greet it or fight with it – I never knew what. She pulled the leash from Regan's little hands and he immediately ran across the street after her. That was it! In seconds Regan was hit by a passing car and suffered a critical head injury and a broken leg. The elderly woman driving the car stopped immediately. She was so overcome that she couldn't drive and I finished up driving her car to the nearest hospital while she cuddled my child on the back seat. I found out later that she never drove a car again.

Angela and I lived at the hospital almost continually for a month while the doctors performed a series of operations to save my little boy's life. They failed and he died three days before what would have been his sixth birthday.

It was my fault. He was too small to hold the lead of such a large dog. I should never have given it to him. I could never feel close to Angela again after causing our son's death.

We both immersed ourselves in our work to keep the pain and in my case the guilt from consuming our lives. I also found that drinking numerous glasses Jack Daniels No 7 was a wonderful way to dull the pain not that it did anything for the rest of my life. It certainly did nothing to assist my deteriorating relationship with Angela or my job.

Despite the best efforts of Angela and the police force I eventually lost them both. I can't remember the details very well – it was all just a horrible protracted period of pain.

After bumming around the country for about six months living in cheap hotels and bars I eventually decided that I was ready for something new. I decided to go on a trip to Africa for a change of scene. When my money was running low, I took a job doing what I did best, I joined the South African Police Force. I didn't realize at the time that I was signing on to a civil war but it kept my mind away from my past and I had nothing to lose. I was recognized for my courage in many of the operations in which I became involved in. Little did they know how easy it is to be courageous when you are feeling suicidal?

I was based in Cape Town and rented an apartment on the hillside looking south. The view was breathtaking but it was very windy. Still from behind the window it was sheer delight to sit and watch the world go by on the all too few occasions when I was off duty and awake.

It is a beautiful country and full of beautiful people both black and white. It was astounding the way racial hatred and suspicion could turn decent people into animals – in fact worse than animals.

When it all finished up and Mandela came to power I decided that it was time to move on. Not that I disagreed with what he was doing – quite the opposite, in fact, but many of my fellow officers saw it differently and so did my supervisors. As a decorated white officer of the old regime, proving my commitment to the new South Africa whilst not impossible would be a challenge. I had reached a point in my life where I could face down my past and explore a new future. So, I resigned from the RSA Police Force and took my pension in a lump sum.

I decided to go back to Australia and I converted my Rand to Australian Dollars while the Rand still had some value. Perth was the nearest place to South Africa and I decided to settle there. I was not sure that I could face returning to Brisbane. I bought a house in Mundaring in the hills behind the city near the Weir. It is almost like living in England and I settled into the quiet community. Some people described me as a hermit because I avoided socializing with the very nice people at the Mundaring Pub as I was determined not to get back into that boozing scene again. By dumb luck, I happened to invest my nest egg in the Australian share market just at a time when the market had taken a hit. The subsequent recovery along with my computing skills allowed me to turn my finances to the point where my investment income was such that I didn't really need to work anymore.

I was getting bored so I joined a computing company whose offices were on the 23rd floor of the Bank West Building. My office had a spectacular view from this building that had been built by Alan Bond, the tycoon who made billions of dollars from the Australian business world before his empire collapsed and he went to jail. I was employed to consult to the many mining companies who were clients of the computer company to use their computer system to identify fraud or avenues by which fraud could be carried out.

In such a profitable industry governed by engineers, metallurgists and chemists but with very few having an understanding of criminal investigation, there was ample scope for shysters to find a niche in the cash flow and divert funds in a myriad of ways. The traditional way to uncover this type of fraud is to establish benchmarks and look for a financial entity that has bad statistics. This works brilliantly in a bank or a similar organization where there is a lot of similar activity going on and comparisons are relatively easy. The variances soon point the way to the opportunist who thinks that he or she has discovered a scam that nobody has thought of before. It is not surprising that many employees succumb to the temptation to syphon away some cash from the millions of dollars passing under their noses each day. These foolish people inevitably finish up in jail. Banks readily and frequently prosecute but are eager to keep this from the media.

But in mining with so many different types of operation, the process of monitoring cost centers is much less effective. I studied the company's comprehensive computer system carefully trawling through the accounting system, the payroll system and the materials management system to identify methods that I could use to beat the system to steal some cash or other valuable resources. Having done that, I would look through the client systems for evidence that some other user had come up with the same idea.

It didn't take long to put my skills to use, I was investigating for a large Indonesian client when I discovered a nice little scam where employees of a coal mine in that country were ordering goods in Rupiah but paying in US Dollars at the Rupiah price. Then they would reset the currency flag after the transaction was completed. The result was that certain vendors were getting paid 6000 times what they should, such was the exchange rate at the time. What was interesting was that of the thousands of vendors supplying the company; only five were repeatedly encountering the same "mistake". An even greater coincidence was that further investigations revealed that all five of these companies were owned by the father in law of the supply manager.

I was asked to travel to Indonesia to consult to the company in chasing down this problem. Once the guilty employees were tracked down they were quietly sacked and made to give up some of the money that they had stolen. Likewise, the vendors were threatened with prosecution unless they refunded some funds also. Overall however crime did pay for the individuals involved as the company did not want the bad publicity and my company did not want to advertise the fact that their software could be cheated.

I found that I enjoyed working in Indonesia and eventually left the computer company and became a freelance consultant providing services to many mining companies throughout the country. I learnt to speak the language of the country. The word for language in this lexicon is "Bahasa" so to be correct one should say that one is speaking "Bahasa Indonesia" I also expanded my skills to include working with a German IT system which provided even more opportunities for fraud. I developed a reputation for being able to find the places where corporate finances were being bled and for being very efficient in plugging the leak. I had developed a network of friends amongst CIOs and security managers of most of the major mining companies in the country.

Under the Suharto presidency the country was stable and the mining companies prospered. The Suharto family had devised a myriad of ways to extract money from the companies and, provided that they played the game, they still did OK. One of my favorite little scams that the family came up with was to impose a government legislated monopoly on gas bottles. Gas bottles, as a result, became hugely expensive in the country. Electricity was also expensive (another scam) and unreliable. The companies had to go along with this and installed the bottles in all their residences and paid the fee.

Then came the overthrow of the President. This made it a very dangerous time to live in the cities especially Jakarta. Life on the mine sites was relatively undisturbed as the local corruption of the police and military that operated in those areas saved the day. The military was disinclined to allow anybody to disrupt their source of graft. Along with the police, they put down civil unrest in the provinces very swiftly.

Suharto was replaced as president by the much-maligned Habibie. This president was in a similar position to Gorbachov of Russia in that he was trying to be the agent of a change for the better but he was rapidly losing the trust of all parties.

The order and enforced stability of the Suharto era was, by then, but a memory. Buildings stood part completed and bridges that were under construction had a couple of spans over a river where the project had stopped. Rusting steel reinforcing rod poked out from ends of concrete slabs like the bones from a rotting corpse.

And this was my life. I moved from mine site to mine site watching the seething mass of different cultures, political parties, religions, government agencies and corporations twist and turn in an endless wrestle for power and money. It was never hard to find the scams and frequently when one went from one company to another one would find the exact same scam being perpetrated at the new location. Usually in days, and even hours in one case, after arriving on site I would have identified the culprits and set about to initiate their arrest.

The fate of the perpetrators depended on their connections. This would range from mere dismissal from the company to being handed to the local military where they would "disappear" never to be heard of again. In some cases, I would be called upon to give evidence in court when the mining company was strong enough to engage police support to prosecute these shysters. There was one current case in which my evidence was going to be critical in securing a prosecution of some very corrupt government officials. Unfortunately for the mining company, PT Copper Co, the perpetrators have friends in both the security forces and the government who are ensuring that the case is dragging in the courts and is unlikely to be tried for at least a year from now.

All this is very good for me and I can literally name my own fee. My share portfolio back in Australia continues to grow. Accommodation is always provided which is not only free but is usually the best that the site can offer. Most times I have been able to engage a "housekeeper" to look after me and to keep me from getting lonely.

I am a pretty happy guy.

Chapter 6 – Tana Toraja

Laurie and Leni rested in the drain pipe for the rest of the morning but by 2:00pm, they were getting hungry. Their bodies were sore all over from the battering that they had suffered from the crash and their escape. Leni's elbow was particularly painful and both were still coughing from to their exposure to the smoke.

They climbed up the hill from which the pipe emerged to see where they were. They had decided that they would just have to take a chance on finding somebody who would assist them rather than somebody who would hand them over to the Government. They both knew of people who had disappeared when taken in by Kopassus and they certainly didn't want to be found by them. Still, hiding in a drain pipe for the rest of their lives was not an option.

Running along the top of the hill was a track which seemed to be a service road for the extensive network of rice paddies that covered the area. The pair of strangers began to walk along the track when they saw a golf buggy being driven towards them.

The buggy was being driven by a woman who appeared to be in her early forties she was accompanied by a young lad who would have been in his early teens. Both were wearing levis and running shoes. The boy wore a black tee shirt with a gold colored circle on the front with the Batman logo on it. The woman had a band in her hair made up of multi colored beads and gold colored, metal blocks. She wore a high necked red long sleeved blouse with a flat beaded necklace with geometric patterns in the beading. The colors were predominately red but there were many other colors as well. She was lightly framed but with the wiry look of a woman who was no stranger to hard work. She obviously wore nothing under her blouse as evidenced by the considerable activity that took place under the light fabric of her well filled blouse whenever she moved. Her levis were faded and worn. This was obviously not to conform to current fashion fads but were obviously the outcome of hard work. Her Nike shoes though still sound also showed signs of wear and staining.

"Who did that?" she asked accusingly as she pointed to the thick smoke rising from the wreckage now hidden behind the hill. "Was it you?" She was obviously very angry that someone would light a fire in her paddy field.

"We didn't do it." Leni replied, replying in Bahasa Indonesian as the woman had done, "Let us show you what happened."

They walked back towards the wreckage until it came into view while the couple followed them in the buggy. "We were passengers on that plane and it got shot down." Leni exclaimed with frustration, anger and desperation in her voice.

The woman and her son looked at the wreckage and her face softened as she turned to face Leni to ask if she was OK. She used the word "sayangku" meaning "my dear" and there was compassion and concern in her voice.

Laurie was surprised and rather anxious when Leni had suggested that they had been shot down to someone who they didn't know but there was no going back on it now.

"Are there other survivors," she asked.

Leni shook her head and her eyes filled with tears.

"What makes you think that it was shot down? The woman asked.

Laurie replied and described the circumstances of the crash and the subsequent visit by the Skyhawk.

"Nothing that this Government does surprises me." The woman replied vehemently.

They were safe; this lady was not a Government supporter. Whether this dislike would extend to her assisting the couple remained to be seen.

They had both been through a traumatic event, moreover, they hadn't eaten and had been walking in the hot sun. Both were starting to feel rather unsteady and clearly the situation was worse for Leni. She attempted to sit on the ground but she fainted just as she began to sit and collapsed and fell sprawled out face down on the ground.

The woman jumped out of her seat and crouched beside the unconscious woman. She rolled her over and sat her up. In the meantime, Laurie sat and rested his back against the wheel of the buggy.

She said "water" and motioned for her son to bring a bottle from a basket mounted on the rear of the buggy.

As she splashed water on Leni's face and then she gently offered her some to sip as she regained consciousness, she pointed to Laurie and told her son to, "Give some to him."

It would be overstating to say that they had recovered but they were eventually able to sit in the buggy. It had only two seats. The rear area was used for stacking produce as well as a variety of equipment and, of course, water.

Laurie was sitting in the driver's seat and the woman asked, "Can you drive?"

"Yes – thank you," he replied, "but what is your name?"

"Ruth." She replied, "This is my son, his name is David"

"Another question, if I may, where are we?

"Tana Toraja" she replied as she walked away.

"Toraja land," Leni whispered, "I have always wanted to visit this place."

There was no further conversation as the mother and son walked ahead along the track leading back to their home while the exhausted couple followed in the buggy. Both were quite astounded and extremely grateful for the courtesy and kindness which had been extended to them.

Chapter 7 – Getting to Know the Family

Ruth led them to her house and introduced them to her mother. She explained to the dignified but frail old woman how they had met and about the shooting down of the aircraft. It was obvious that the mother was the respected leader of the family but that it was Ruth who made everything happen.

Laurie was surprised that they spoke in English but, as they found out later, their hosts had their own complex variety of languages and dialects and that they also spoke Bahasa Indonesia because it was the mandatory national language of the country. They spoke English because, as Ruth explained, "it was best for education, trade and watching TV".

They were never introduced to the mother by name and so Laurie addressed her as "Ma'am" which everyone seemed to think was quite appropriate. The aged matriarch shook her head in disgust when she heard about the plane being shot down. She spoke in a voice that was frail and with a Dutch accent when she spoke to the group and looked directly at her daughter, "The Makassarese Muslims killed your grandfather years before you were born." Ruth looked back at her mother with respect but with a twist to her mouth that said, "I've heard all this many time before."

"We must all be careful," the old lady continued, "ever since these jihadists infiltrated the military, their tentacles of terror have spread right through this country and beyond."

Leni nodded her head in enthusiastic agreement.

"Tell me about yourself Mr. Australian." The old lady asked Laurie with a laugh in her voice indicating that she recognized his accent. So, he began to tell his story. He tried to be concise but she would have none of that and kept asking questions every time that she felt that he had left something out. She even drew out, how he had lost Regan and Angela and her old eyes became tearful as he described this most painful time of his life.

Then, it was Leni's turn and she had fewer interruptions because she had seen from Laurie's experience that the old woman wanted the full story and so she did not omit any detail.

Finally, after her story came to an end, the old lady with puzzlement in her voice said, "But you didn't tell me how you two met?"

"We only met this morning when we sat beside each other on the plane that crashed." Laurie replied.

"You look so good together, I thought that you were lovers." She laughed.

Laurie looked at Leni and saw that she was looking at him. She was blushing.

The old matriarch continued, "We are Toraga, we are proud of who we are and we are no friends to those, including this government, who have long been jealous of our culture and who have attacked us for hundreds of years. Yet, we are proud of our hospitality and we always extend it to strangers. You are welcome to stay with us until you can safely leave. As our guests, you are free to go anywhere in our village but I suggest that you stay close to this house because people will see you out and about and they might talk to the authorities who may be looking for you."

"Thank you, Ma'am, I am most grateful, most grateful indeed." The tall Australian replied

Leni bowed and displayed the submissive politeness so typical of Asian women as she also thanked her elderly host.

She then looked at young David and said, "take Mr …." And she paused before asking, "What is your name?"

"Laurie Harris," he replied, "But my friends all call me Truck"

The old woman looked puzzled but Ruth got it. "A lorry is a truck" she explained to her mother. Her mother began to laugh at the joke.

She again spoke to David and again said, "take Mr Truck Harris to the bathroom and can you find some clean clothes for him to wear."

Then she focused on Leni and asked, what is your name dear?"

"Leni Hong, Ma'am" she replied.

"No funny nicknames?" She asked laughing.

"'fraid not," she replied looking at Laurie grinning.

"Ruth, please take care of Miss Hong."

Bowing again, Leni said, "Please call me Leni."

David took Laurie to a part of the large house where the unattached boys and men lived. Laurie had the choice of a shower or a bath. Although, he almost always showered, he chose to fill the bath with water as hot as he could stand and then relaxed in it to sooth the many bruises around his body.

What he really wanted to do was to close his eyes and doze off in the comfort of the hot bath but David, who insisted in calling him Mr. Truck, gave him rock star treatment and really wanted to chat to him.

Eventually the lad disappeared while carrying Laurie's soiled and torn clothes away but after quite some time, he returned with a bright red shirt with traditional motifs patterned on it. He also produced a pair of levis. As it turned out, they were too small and too short but he was able to squeeze into them with difficulty. There was also a pair of boxer undershorts which were also too small.

David escorted him to a bunk where, after shedding the "new" clothes, he lay naked and decided to get some sleep. David agreed to rouse him when it was time for the family to meet for dinner. He asked the very obliging young lad if he could arrange to bring him a coffee when he woke because he would likely be still very sleepy.

True to his promise, David did wake Laurie about two hours later with a cup of black coffee. He proudly announced that it was grown by the village and it is the best coffee in the world. Obviously, the lad had not seen much of the world, but the coffee was strong and quite pleasant to taste. Laurie thanked him for his kindness and again squeezed into the levis and went to dinner.

Laurie met Leni as each was each being escorted to the dinner room she was accompanied by Ruth. Leni was also wearing borrowed clothes. She wore a short denim skirt and her blouse was similarly patterned in traditional motifs like the shirt that Laurie was wearing. It became obvious as soon as she moved that she was also no longer wearing a bra. Whether this was a widespread Toraja custom or merely the fashion preference of just the females of this family, Laurie couldn't tell but it was certainly not something that he had any difficulty with.

She smiled when she saw Laurie, obviously, she noticed his tight jeans and her eyes were drawn to the obvious bulge at his crotch. "Is that a gun that you are carrying or are you just happy to see me" she asked laughing. Young David was obviously too young to be aware of the famous Mae West quote but the older sister whose name I later discovered was Naomi laughed.

Leni had her right arm in a sling and Laurie asked if her elbow was feeling better.

Leni looked to Naomi and said, "Yes! Naomi helped me. She put ice packs on it and gave me some ibuprofen to stop the inflammation. Putting it in a sling helps stop me moving it which will make it hurt less and speed up the recovery. Naomi is very good at healing people."

Naomi was an attractive young woman of about fifteen years of age. She was beaming with pride at

Leni's acknowledgment of her first aid skills. She had a wide face and a small nose which seemed to be a characteristic of the Torajan ethnicity. Her shining black hair had a slight wave to it unlike the very straight hair of most Indonesians and also of the Chinese women like Leni. Her lithe young body was just beginning to indicate the development of her womanhood.

They got to the dining area just as Ruth senior walked in through a door at the opposite side of the room. She smiled enthusiastically and welcomed them to dine. She expressed amusement at Laurie's sartorial predicament and said, "We have taken note of your clothing size and Ruth has ordered some replacements over the web. These should be delivered tomorrow afternoon. We have also washed and have done our best to repair the clothes that you were wearing when you arrived. They will be dry enough for you to put back on in the morning. I hope that you don't mind us taking over like this."

"Of course not, we are very grateful." Said Leni before Laurie could get a word in and so he just nodded in agreement.

"Can I pay you?" Laurie managed to ask.

"Probably best that you look after what cash that you have because you will need it to get back to Australia. If you use your credit card, then they will know that you are alive. Besides which, you are our guests – we are very happy to look after you until we figure out how to get you away safely."

Another daughter burst into the room. Her name, as they later learnt, was Rachel. She was wearing a Star Wars tee shirt which had a similar level of activity bouncing around underneath it as did her mother's. She was also wearing very tight levi pants which was seeming to be the family uniform.

The attractive young woman was panting and said, "There are soldiers and other men on the beach. They are gathering up the wreckage of the crashed plane and putting it on a boat."

"Did they see you?" asked the old woman.

"I don't think so." The girl replied. "You know how the beach is hidden from the track by the edge of the dune…"

"Of course, I know!" cut in the old woman leaving Rachel with her hands in the air as she was clumsily trying to indicate the topography of the beach and the road in the air.

"Were there any other survivors?"

"None that I could see."

"What about the bodies?"

"they were being put in boxes."

"coffins?"

"No – they were just boxes."

"This is what we are up against. These people have no decency. Innocent people died on that flight and they will never find the spirit world. Their bodies will be disrespected and their families will be left to grieve, never knowing what happened to their loved ones."

"It gets worse, Grandmother, there were many items of luggage that survived without damage and the soldiers were looting them and dividing up the clothes, computers and cameras amongst themselves."

"You were lucky that you weren't seen. I hate to think what would have happened to you if you had been spotted and captured. These people are animals."

Laurie had to speak, "Ma'am," he said, "Nobody in this room is more disgusted by what has happened to that plane and to us. But I must say that I have worked with many soldiers and security people in this great archipelago, for decades, and there are many fine wonderful people, present company included, that live here. We must not allow the actions of a corrupt and evil minority to poison our thoughts to everyone outside our own group."

"You are a good man, Truck," she replied. "But we Toraja have been mistreated for hundreds of years and we need to be ever vigilant to defend our culture against those who strive to destroy it."

"My family is not like them." Said Leni, speaking softly.

"No, my dear," the old lady replied, "the *Orang Tionghoa-Indonesia* have suffered just as much as we have by the Javanese insiders."

Ruth interjected, "The best thing that we can do now, is make our guests as comfortable as possible and help them get safely away when the opportunity arises. For the moment, our dinner is getting cold. Please let's just eat now." She looked at her mother in apology at interrupting her intense observations.

The old lady smiled at her daughter's diplomacy and nodded.

The meal was delicious. It was a very spicy dish called Papiong which was made up of pork and rice which had been broiled over hot coals in large bamboo tubes.

The family gathered to eat and as conversation continued and questions were asked, the two outsiders learnt some details about this family that fate had cast them into. Ruth's husband, named Harold, is a civil engineer and was employed by a construction company in Bali. He gets back to the village one weekend per month and sometimes can take a couple of weeks' holiday at home with his family. There is also an older brother, named Joshua, who is a senior IT manager at the Freeport Gold mine in Irian Jaya. It turned out that Laurie had met Joshua on a previous visit to the mine. Rachel was just finishing her degree in mining engineering and would be looking for a job in the new year.

"It must be tough having your husband and family move away to work." Leni commented to Ruth.

"It is," the mother replied, "but there is not much money to be made growing rice and some coffee. We need to bring some money into the family and my husband and his clever children..." she paused and smiled at Rachel, "... can get work in other parts of the country to support the village life."

"As long as they never forget that they are Toraja and we are their family and this is their home. That is what Matthew thinks and I agree with him," stated the Grandmother vehemently and the visitors noticed some surreptitious smiles around the table as they listened once again to the message that they had obviously heard many times before.

The meal became more relaxed and Leni asked Rachel, "Who is Matthew?"

"He is my grandfather," Rachel replied, "He went to sleep two months ago, and he is waiting to go to the spirit world. Would you like to meet him?"

Both of the guests had heard of the famous funeral rites of the Toraja but Leni in particular knew very little about them. Nonetheless, both, Laurie and Leni were a little afraid of what they might be letting themselves into but in gratitude for their hospitality they agreed to go along with it.

"Yes, OK." Leni said nervously and Laurie nodded in agreement,

The meal went on for a couple of hours and "Mr Truck" as the younger family members had come to call him, recounted some stories from his past particularly those about his life as a police officer and they all laughed as he described how sheer stupidity had led to the arrest of some of the criminals who he had sent to jail.

The old woman eventually stood to indicate that she was ready to retire and after being hugged by the family she walked to the door through which she had entered earlier.

"Grandmother," said Rachel respectfully, Truck and Leni have asked to pay their respects to my Grandfather."

"Oh, that is very nice! He will be glad to see you," the matriarch replied. "Do come with me."

She led them through the door to a walkway which ran as far as the steps leading up into the building. It was covered by a roof made of palm leaves. The building was spectacular as were the other twenty or so similar buildings that held key positions around the village.

The building was constructed mostly from bamboo and was shaped like a saddle with a concave roof which curled up to a very high front and rear rather like the bow of a traditional wooden boat.

"Many villages have been built with the tongkonans all very close together," the woman said as she ascended the stairs with a confidence that belied her age. "When our ancestors built here, they had plenty of room so they spaced them out. This was good as it turned out because, as the family grew, we were able to build other western style houses in between.

"Why don't you build more houses like this?" Leni asked.

"Western houses are cheaper to build and need less maintenance." She replied. "All families must have a nice big tongkonan to show their status. Ours is the biggest and the best - as it should be."

Laurie had noticed the other tongkonans in the village as Ruth had escorted them in earlier that day. They all looked pretty spectacular to him, but if his elderly host thought that hers was the biggest and the best, he was not about to argue with her.

They went inside and were escorted to a large room at the opposite end of the building. On entering the room, they were confronted with a horrible sight. There was a chair with a bright red tapestry covering the back and extending over the seat. The tapestry had a considerable amount of gold trim and was embroidered with the now familiar traditional Toraja motifs. At either side of the chair was a parasol of the same red color and embroidery as the seat cover. Seated on this chair was a corpse. He was wearing a traditional red shirt and levis. On his lap was an old Dell laptop and his right hand held a rifle. He was wearing glasses which accentuated the horrible eye sockets with desiccating shrunken eyes only partially concealed by the equally deteriorated eyelids. His facial tissues had shrunken and had pulled his lips away from his teeth. This gave the appearance that he was smiling.

"Grandad is dressed and is holding the things that he loves." Rachel commented.

Leni gasped when she saw this gruesome sight and Laurie grabbed her hand and squeezed it to reassure her and hopefully dissuade her from reacting.

"Matthew sits there and sleeps while he waits for us to send him to the land of souls." The old woman said as she pointed to a bed close by and said, "I sleep here where I can be close to him."

"We had better go now," said Rachel. "Sleep well, Grandad and Grandma, I will see you in the morning.

Laurie picked up on the belief and said, "Goodnight Sir and Ma'am, sleep well."

"Goodnight, the elderly matron replied, "Rachel, do show our friends out."

As we walked out she explained that the entire family used to live in the tongkonan but stopped doing it about twenty years ago, when the western house was built. The family now all live in the western house except for her Grandfather and Grandmother.

"Why do you now choose to live in a western style house?" Leni asked.

"It is easier to build bathrooms and air-conditioning in a western style house?" Rachel answered.

She pointed to an assortment of buffalo horns mounted at the front of the tongkonan.

"We place a horn there whenever someone who lives there goes to the land of souls." She explained.

Laurie counted Twenty-two horns mounted on the wall.

As the three walked back from the extraordinary building with its even more extraordinary contents, the two visitors exchanged glances which were noticed by the perceptive Rachel.

As they entered the dining room Rachel invited them to sit at the table and join her in a coffee. They sat and made small talk as the percolator chuffed and spat before Rachel poured three cups and then sat with the two bemused visitors.

"Look!" the beautiful young Torajan woman exclaimed, "I know that you find our beliefs strange – probably confronting and I want to talk things through with you."

"You don't have to, "Leni replied, "Your beliefs are your beliefs, there is no need to explain them to us and I am in no way critical of them."

Laurie interjected, "You are lucky, I don't have any religious beliefs and I envy those who do for the comfort that they bring to them."

"But we expect you to be with us for a few weeks and I want you to understand what is going on." Rachel said earnestly. "Do you have any questions that you want me to answer?"

"OK," said Leni, "You say that you are Christian and so am I, but none of this death stuff is in the bible."

"I am a Christian," Rachel replied, "but it is in the bible. Jesus himself rose from the dead and so did Lazarus."

Laurie broke in, and said, "I am in no position to have a theological discussion on this and I just totally accept that you folk are entitled to your beliefs, but can you tell us what is going to happen while we are here – and again I must thank you for your kindness and hospitality."

Well," said Rachel, Next week, we will be sending my grandfather to the land of souls. There is nothing for you to do except watch and enjoy the food. There will be many of our ancestors who will be brought back from their place of rest to celebrate his passage…"

Leni interrupted, "Their bodies – you mean."

"Well – Yes! But we believe that the spirit remains close to the earthly remains and returns when it is moved to again be part of its family and friends. We are not sad about death, it is a time of great rejoicing as we send our loved one to join the spirits of his family and friends."

"OK! Well, I am looking forward to next week." Said Laurie. Leni said nothing.

The village was a hive of activity during the week and there was a procession of visitors wanting to talk to Matthew and Ruth senior. Leni managed to find out that the family had a tradition of naming the firstborn female in each family "Ruth". There was no confusion because they were referred to by their family titles, except for Rachel's older sister who will be called Ruth until she becomes a mother. Depending on the circumstances at the time, the current mother's title would become Grandmother and the Grandmother would become Great Grandmother all titles would be spoken in the native Toraja language.

It was agreed that it was becoming pointless to continue to attempt to hide Laurie and Leni. With the festivities, it was thought best that Leni should wear a traditional Torajan costume and young Naomi delighted in cutting and setting Leni's hair in typical Torojan style.

She was slightly taller than the Torojan women who are all rather petite but not so much that she was noticed. Her skin color was slightly paler than that of her hosts but again, not so much that she stood out. The only problem was her Asian eyes which they solved by having her wear a pair of very cool looking Ray Bans which any Torojan girl would certainly wear if she could.

Laurie was more of a problem. His height and skin color ruled out any hope of making him look like a Torojan. They decided to try to pass him off as an American tourist. His new Levis arrived on the second day as promised and the family rummaged about to find a very large camera for him to wear along with a tee shirt which was printed with 'Lynchburg TN Home of Jack Daniels' along with a picture of a bottle of Old No 7. He decided to call himself Earl Rodgers and to attempt to speak with as good an American accent as he could manage. The family and Laurie thought that his fake accent was good enough to fool the Torojans, but would be unlikely to fool any Americans whom he might meet. It was not unusual to have tourists at funerals although it was not encouraged by this family. But a tourist would not be out of place.

Laurie and Leni saw very little of each other in the ensuing days; particularly as Leni became more involved with the women in decorating the house and the tongkonan. She got used to working around Matthew and was no longer spooked by his sightless eyes. Laurie assisted in herding the water buffalo and pigs and remembered to take lots of photographs when he was outside. Actually, the camera was quite a good one and he took lots of photos because the whole activity was fascinating. The two did not sit together at the dinner table but sat with family groups of their own sex. Laurie thought that it was odd and was disappointed that Leni seemed to be deliberately distancing herself from him.

The family grew larger as absent members returned to the village. This included Ruth's husband, Harold, and the eldest brother Joshua whom Laurie had met on an earlier trip to Freeport. It needed to be explained to Joshua, very quickly, why they were calling Laurie 'Earle' and Joshua was very supportive.

They also got to meet the eldest daughter Ruth Junior and her boyfriend Rudy.

The first day of the funeral which was a Sunday did not involve Matthew and Grandmother Ruth who were still in the tongkonan. Many older women were with her and talked and laughed to raise the widow's mood and reinforce the mode of joy at Matthews's journey to the spirit world.

On the second funeral day, the *Ma'randing* warrior dance was performed to praise the courage of the deceased during life. Harold and Joshua along with senior men from the other households performed the dance. Each had a sword and a large shield made from buffalo skin. They each wore a very ornate and colorful uniform which was heavily ornamented with items that were reminiscent of the events that occurred in the long history of the culture. The uniform included a helmet with a buffalo horn. Laurie thought it incongruous to see this young man whom he had previously known as a software developer engaged in this dance in which he metamorphosed as a fearsome warrior.

After the dance and a lot of speeches by various people including a highly decorated old woman who was some sort of high priestess, Matthew was brought out accompanied by his wife.

The elder women, led by Ruth, the daughter, perform the *Ma'katia* dance while singing a poetic song and wearing a most beautiful costume of long feathers. As the dance continued, Rachel who was standing closely beside Laurie explained that the *Ma'katia* dance was being performed to remind the audience of the generosity and loyalty of her grandfather.

Then came a part of the ceremony that was shocking in its brutality and horror.

Approximately ten water buffalo were herded out. Each was led by a handler who had a short rope attached to the nose ring that each beast was fitted with. The animals were obviously frightened by the noise and the large number of people present. The handlers spoke soothingly to their charges. The beasts responded to their handler and seemed to trust them. Each was led to an open area in the center of the assembled crowd, the handler was given a large sharp knife with a heavy blade rather like a machete. Each handler held the nose of his beast high before whacking the knife into the exposed throat of the beast. Some buffalo jumped back when they felt the impact and the pain of the sharp blade imbedding into its neck but many in their docility and innocence simply stood quietly as their life blood gushed out.

This slaughter was followed by the skinning and butchering of the carcasses. There was much glee by the many who participated in the process. They were wading in the blood of the animals which pooled on the ground.

The large amounts of meat were carried away to the houses where it was to be cooked, a similar process ensued with a collection of pigs. Many of the handlers were women who participated with similar vigor and expertise as the men. Their job was more difficult however because the pigs proved to be less docile than were the buffalo.

This bloody ceremony took a couple of hours to complete. Many buckets of water were brought out to flush away the blood. This was ineffectual but it cleared the area sufficiently for group of boys and girls to perform an energetic and happy hand clapping dance which was called the *Ma'dondan*.

Later women appeared from the surrounding houses. Laurie could not tell if every house was involved in preparing the feast – certainly there were few, if any, who did not play a role.

What followed was an orgy of consumption. There was much of the local Ballo, which is made from palm wine to drink along with the Indonesian beer, Bintang. Laurie noticed that the younger people including Rachel who never seemed be very far from him seemed to prefer the Bintang.

There was much dancing after the feast which went late into the night.

Leni had had as much of a good time as she could handle and found her way alone into the house and collapsed into her bunk. She sobbed quietly to herself because she desperately wanted to dance with and kiss Laurie to express her desire for him. She just couldn't get the chance because Rachel always seemed to be in her way.

It was an hour later, around 1:00am when Laurie made his way to his room and collapsed into his bunk.

He was just on the verge of going to sleep when a woman came to his room. She dropped her clothes on the floor and found his bed in the darkness before slithering in naked beside him. He was a little drunk and he had become aroused watching the many young women dancing and so he quickly became erect when this firm young body with her large breasts cuddled up to him. It was dark but he figured that it was Rachel and he whispered her name questioningly. "Yes." She replied as she pressed her body against him and he was acutely aware of her hard nipples pressing against his chest.

"Stop," He said, "I don't have any condoms."

"Don't worry, I am on the pill."

"Are you sure?"

"Yes – do you need me to show you the box?"

"No, I trust you."

"Good!"

She reached down and took his swollen member in her hand and squeezed the tip which had become so engorged that it was hurting. She held him to the slippery entrance of her body and squealed softly in delight as his animal instinct took over and he thrust deeply into her stretching her young sheath until she thought she would burst. She moaned with the delightful pain while he grunted as he repeatedly thrust into her. He enveloped her in his arms and kissed her lips as the delightful orgasmic convulsions took control of his body. The young Torajan gasped as her body responded and soon they lay together panting in each other's arms while his tumescence gradually subsided.

As the first rays of the sun began to light the room, she kissed him and hopped out of the bed. She picked up her discarded clothes and without bothering to put them on, she scampered silently to her room.

The celebrations continued into the following day and through the week. People woke, ate to excess, drank to excess and many made love. During this time, some of the other ancestors had had their bodies removed from their crypts and were cleaned up and dressed and paraded around. Whilst this ghoulish custom revolted the visitors, the locals saw this as perfectly acceptable and, without exception, they talked to the ancestors as if they were still alive.

By the Eleventh day since the funeral began, when the guest of honor was to be laid to rest, the population seemed to be exhausted. It seemed that the food was running out because the banquets had degenerated into snacks and there was no more ballo. Someone had driven to a tavern in a nearby town and brought back a few more cartons of Bintang.

But to Laurie's surprise, the revelers seemed to get a second wind as they began the final part of the ceremony. Matthew's body was placed in a casket which was shaped like the lower portion of a tongkonan. His rifle was placed beside him along with his laptop, also included were some packets of cigarettes and a bag of licorice all sorts which he apparently was very fond of. He was still wearing his glasses. Once that was done the upper portion of the mini tongkonan was placed over him and after yet more speeches and incantations, he was carried along a winding track to the mausoleum which consisted of a series of caves dug into the side of a cliff. With the use of bamboo poles, a great deal of energy, and the experience of having done it before, Matthew's casket was laid to rest in one of the caves. The final step was to place a carved wooden effigy of the man at the entrance of the cave which apparently, he was to share with others in his family.

Finally, after more speeches, more prayers and more incantations Matthew was laid to rest. Or at least he would be until the next funeral when he was likely to be taken out, scrubbed up and paraded about.

As they made their way back, Laurie happened to be walking with Naomi. To make conversation, he asked the young girl what she wanted to do when she grew up. He didn't realize it but he had asked a contentious question that struck a raw nerve with the young woman.

"What I want doesn't matter. I am the youngest daughter. My family have been able to provide Joshua and Rachel with an education and David is a boy so he must be educated also. My parents have told me that I will likely not be able to go to university because they simply can't afford it."

"Are your school marks good?" he asked.

"Last exam, I got A's in all subjects except art. I can't draw for nuts."

"So, what lies ahead for you, do you think?"

"After I finish school, I will work in the village and take over running the farm. I guess I will find a nice man to marry and I will have lots of babies."

What would you do, if you could go to university?"

"I want to be a doctor."

She began to cry. Through her sobs, she said, "I am not angry at my parents – and I guess that they are doing the right thing by warning me of the problem early so that I don't get unrealistic hopes."

They walked on in silence.

Chapter 8 – Time to Move On

Village life returned to normal after the funeral.

At a family dinner two days later, Naomi said that she had been approached by a woman whom she had never seen before and was asked if she had seen anybody around who wasn't part of the community.

"What did you say?" asked Ruth (the mother).

"Only you!" The family around the table laughed.

Ruth (the mother) told everyone to be careful and that Leni and Laurie should stay in the house to avoid being spotted. She had been talking to the district representative of the Regency council during the ceremony. He had told her that the government had told them to be on the lookout for anyone who turned up unexpectedly. They claimed that they were looking for murderers who had escaped police custody. He warned them that these escapees were likely to be claiming to have survived a plane crash.

"Ha!" exclaimed Ruth (the grandmother) angrily, "Just what you would expect of these corrupt lying government dogs. You saw the crashed plane yourselves."

The first reaction about the table was to be relieved to see the old woman getting back to her feisty old self. She had become very quiet an introspective after Matthew was lain to rest and some of the family, especially her daughter, were becoming worried about her.

Laurie spoke up, "Look," he said," I am worried that we are putting your family in danger. I think it best that we get down to Makassar as soon as we can to leave you good folk in peace."

"And what will happen?" asked the old woman, "As soon as you check into a hotel, you will need to show your passport. As soon as Leni says that she doesn't have one, they will investigate why."

"OK!" Laurie replied, "we will accept your hospitality gratefully for a little longer until we figure out a plan."

There was discussion of various impractical ways in which they might be able to escape before the family went their separate ways leaving Leni and Laurie alone at the table.

"I think that you should go to Ujung Pandang by yourself," Leni said, referring to the city of Makassar by its traditional name.

"Why?" Laurie asked.

"Because they are not after you. You can just use your Australian passport and get a flight back to Australia and be safe."

"And what about you?"

"I will be OK, you got me out of the crash but now you must look after yourself."

"You will not be OK. They are after you and if you don't get out of this country, you will finish up in a prison cell or worse."

"That may be but it is not your problem."

"It is my problem."

"Why?"

"Because I care about you. I want to help you to survive."

"How can that be, you are sweet on Rachel. I see how she follows you around. For all I know, you might be sleeping with her."

"Leni, I have slept with many women. Maybe one day, you might even let me sleep with you. But regardless of that, I can tell you one thing; if I get out of this country and I have not secured your safety, I will be haunted by that for the rest of my life."

"You are a sweet and brave man, Truck. But I don't want you to get killed because of me."

"It is not your choice, I'm here for you whether you want me or not."

"Because you don't want me to haunt you."

"I think that you would be a very scary ghost."

She laughed and took his hand and kissed it.

"OK, first there is something that you should know."

"What's that?"

"I have two passports."

"How did you do that?"

"I didn't really have much choice. When I joined the South African police, they insisted that I take out RSA citizenship so I did. Then when I had to travel overseas on police business, I got issued with an RSA passport."

"It is still issued in you name though?"

"Yep!"

"Still," said Leni thinking aloud, "That will be better because they will be alerted to look for an Australian passport."

"So, what will we do to get you out?"

"I don't know but I will call my cousin. She will talk to her husband to see if he can figure something out."

"That's Hendrick, the government guy."

"Wow! You don't miss much."

"I'm trained to – I was a cop."

They hatched a plan to contact Joyce.

First, Laurie hired a taxi and in his American tourist alter ego went to the 7-Eleven store in the nearby town where after buying a few bits and pieces wrote down the number of the public phone that was available there.

Next, they asked Ruth junior to phone Joyce on her mobile to ask her to phone the number at the 7-Eleven. Ruth said that somebody important to her needed help. She gave the number in a code made up of personal details which would be known only to Joyce.

The following day, the girls, Rachel, Naomi and Ruth junior all dressed in their "uniform" of tee shirts, jeans and Ray Bans all drove to the 7-Eleven along with Leni who was also wearing the same outfit. They timed their arrival for five minutes before the call was expected. The three sisters talked loudly and flirted with the guy behind the counter while they fussed around buying stockings and lifting their tee shirts to "decide how they would match their skin color". There was no chance that the poor guy would even have noticed that Leni was even there much less that she quickly snatched up the phone before its first ring had completed.

"Leni?" Hendrick asked.

"yes"

"I know where you are from the phone number. Don't worry this phone is secure. How can I help you?"

"I need a passport."

"I figured that you might. Be at this phone same time in three days, that's Friday, and I will call you back."

"Thanks so much – I love you guys."

"We love you too. Kisses from your cousin."

"Click" he hung up.

The phone call took less than twenty seconds. They guy in the store had no idea that the call had even been made.

Leni went back to the counter and played with the stockings. She chose a pair of panty hose and then asked the girls if they would stand in front of her, "to stop this guy peeking" while she dropped her jeans and put them on. Of course, the guy watched intently and there were 'accidental' gaps in the human screen made by the three sisters.

"I must go home to compare the color with my new skirt," Leni flirted.

I will come back on Friday if that is OK. You will be here won't you Honey she said to the checkout guy. He nodded enthusiastically – too overawed to speak.

As the girls crowded back into the car, they were still giggling. "I swear he got a hard on when Leni took of her jeans." Rachel laughed.

"More importantly, said Ruth with a serious tone, "how did you get on; and what's this about going back on Friday?"

"My cousin will look to get me a passport – he is calling back on that phone on Friday."

"So, we will need to flirt with Mr. Randy again on Friday.

"Yes."

"OK! That will be fun."

When they got back, Leni told Laurie what had happened.

"I don't know what to do if he can't come up with something." Laurie remarked desolately.

Leni hugged him and said, "Don't worry, Trucky, my cousin in law is very clever and well connected."

Laurie didn't hear much of what she said, he was thinking about the way she intimately modified his nickname.

Friday came and the girls went back to the 7-Eleven but this time the two older sisters wore denim skirts while Naomi and Leni wore cotton skirts.

This time the girls pretended that they wanted to try on the panties that were in the store and they tried on various pairs with the full attention of Mr. Randy as they now all referred to him as.

Leni again picked up the phone on the first ring.

"Leni?"

"Yes."

"I can't get you a new passport but I am sending your cousin's. You both look sufficiently alike to get past normal security."

"I don't want to get her into trouble."

"Let me know when you are safe and I will report it as stolen."

"When will you post it?"

"I already have. It is in a carving that says Happy Birthday Ruth. Split it open. I have sent it care of the 7-Eleven store."

"Great thanks! I will call you when I am safe. Love you."

"Love you too!"

'Click'

Leni went to the counter where the sisters were still titillating poor Mr. Randy.

"Hey!" she said, "my boyfriend is sending me a present and I have asked him to send it to me care of this store."

"Why don't you just get him to send it to your house?" asked Mr. Randy.

"Because I don't want our mother to know."

Picking up the cue, Rachel said, "Oh no! she would get so angry." Then she placed her hand on his and asked him to phone her on her mobile when the present arrived.

Of course, he agreed and she wrote her number on a pad that he very hastily provided.

"I hope that you didn't mind giving him your number." Leni said apologetically.

"Not at all, he is kind of cute," the uninhibited sister replied laughing.

It took two days before Rachel ran to find Leni. "Your parcel has arrived. I have arranged to go and pick it up for you."

"Shouldn't I come with you?"

"No, we don't want him looking at you too closely and besides I want to have some fun with Mr. Randy."

Laurie and Leni were waiting together and eagerly anticipating getting the package when Rachel returned driving in at a dangerously high speed.

"Your package from your secret admirer." She said as she handed it to Leni.

"The boy at the 7-Eleven won't talk, will he? Laurie asked.

"I asked him to keep it to himself so our mother wouldn't find out. Then I kissed him and the cheeky bugger grabbed a feel of my tits. He won't talk. He is waiting for me to go back and I just might – seeing as nothing is happening here." She remarked looking at Laurie pointedly.

Leni tore open the package. There was a carving of a large wooden heart with a lovely card that said, "Dearest Barbara, I am giving my heart to you love Allan."

She threw away the card and looked at the carving. On very close inspection, she noticed that the carving was made from two pieces of wood glued together.

Laurie looked around and eventually came back with a large solid carving knife and a piece of wood. He placed the knife on the join of the two halves and tapped the back edge of the knife firmly. After a few taps, it had sunk about 10mm into the wood. Nothing else happened.

Then he repeated the action on the other side.

Still nothing happened.

Then he rested the heart upside down resting on the two rounded sections.

He rested the knife on the join at the point of the heart and tapped again. Because the wood was narrow at that point the knife sunk down about 20mm with only three taps. With one more tap the wood split such that

Laurie was able to grab the two halves and pull mightily to separate them.

Both halves had been hollowed out sufficiently to accommodate a passport.

Leni hugged Laurie before snatching up the document and opening it. A slip of paper fell out. She picked it up and read the short text written in Bahasa Indonesian. Translated it said:

Best wishes my lady

Good luck

Ujang

She could imagine the big man carefully carving out the wooden heart to protect the cousin of his beloved mistress. Tears came to Leni's eyes.

Laurie looked at the passport carefully. Joyce did resemble Leni and the photo would likely pass casual scrutiny. He doubted very much if she could get past Australian immigration with such a dubious photograph.

He explained this to Leni who was crestfallen and tried to dispute the bad news that he was trying to convey.

"But you white guys can't tell us Asians apart." She argued.

"Some white guys can't but the people on immigration are very good." I know, I have worked with them.

"So, what do we do?" she asked sobbing with disappointment.

"Don't give up, I've got a bit of a plan."

"What are you going to do?"

"First I need to get on the web."

"What then?"

"Then, you will go and talk to "Mother" and see if she can help you to relax, maybe with a good slug of ballo."

They both went to see Ruth, the mother, who logged on to her laptop and, passing it to him, said "Here, Truck, send what you like."

Laurie thanked her very warmly for this great act of trust and settled down to send a message. He also asked her to look after Leni.

Later he came back and said, I've sent an email to my mate at Freeport. I don't know if I have remembered his email address correctly or if he will respond but I have given it a shot.

They sat and talked to "Mother" for an hour or more before she stood and said, it's time that I went to bed.

After she left, Leni asked when he thought that his mate will reply.

"If he agrees to reply, he will do it in the morning before he does his rounds of the site."

"Here's hoping," she said as she raised a glass with the last remaining mouthful of ballo.

"Indeed!" responded Laurie, "Now it's time that I went to bed."

"Goodnight Truck, lock your door," she replied, "I have got to know Rachel only too well."

Laurie laughed.

He was awoken at 6:30am by banging on his door. It was "Mother". "I have got a reply from your friend at Freeport – come and look."

"Turn around," he said as he pushed down the sheets indicating that he was sleeping naked."

She did and as he pulled his trousers on, he saw her looking at him in the mirror.

He smiled and thought to himself, like daughter, like mother.

They hurried to her office and she extended the chair in front of the keyboard to him and she stood behind watching the monitor.

She read the email that he had sent the night before:

'Hi Johann,

I am in a bit of a bind and I need some help.

Do you have a private email account that I can contact you on?

Cheers

Truck'

The reply simply said 'mobile # for a text please'

Laurie asked 'Mother' if he could give her mobile number and she agreed.

He typed '# is:' and he bent forward and 'Mother' bent over the back of the chair and while resting her breasts on his shoulders, she typed in her phone number.

They looked at each other and wondered if he was still at his PC.

Moments later her phone dinged and an address appeared on the screen.

Jakob_regop10inch@gmail.com.au

Laurie laughed when he saw the email address. He knew that 'Jakob regop' was Afrikaans slang for 'stiff penis'

"What is it? Asked 'Mother' when she heard him laugh.

"You don't want to know."

Because the address finished in .au, Laurie realized that the messages finished at a server in Australia and so they were invisible to Indonesian authorities. He had served with Johann many times while they both worked together in the RSA Police and they had become good friends. He had also worked with him at Freeport on two occasions and had assisted in uncovering a fraud. He knew that Johann was a tough professional who knew what was needed to preserve the security of the Mine site and he did so with ruthless efficiency.

He sent the following message:

Mate!

Trust that all is well with you.

I am in a bit of a bind since I have a girlfriend who is Chinese descent but through no fault of her own, is being chased by the Government.

I need to get out of sight for a while until I figure a way to get her to safety.

Could you possibly arrange for us to come to Freeport for a while?

Cheers

Truck

'Mother' made two cups of coffee while they waited for a response. Laurie kept clicking 'send/receive' from time to time as they made small talk. While they were waiting, Leni entered the room.

"What are you doing?" she asked.

"Truck is emailing his friend at Freeport to help get you out of here."

The young woman looked at the screen and read the messages. It was obvious that Laurie would have preferred to keep the interchange to himself.

Leni read quickly and smiled as she looked at Laurie. "Girlfriend Huh?" she commented laughing.

Suddenly, their attention was riveted to the screen when a reply was received.

Truck,

Let me see what I can do?

What is GFs name and passport #?

Also, where are you?

Johann

Laurie looked at Leni and she scurried away before returning less than a minute later with Joyce's passport in hand. She bent over the chair just as 'Mother' had done a few minutes earlier and typed over his shoulder:

Joyce Herianto
Indonesia Passport # C5874012

Currently in Tana Toraja

Laurie pasted this into an email followed by the words: *skilpad het nie vere nie, en*
appels is nie pere nie.

Without being asked, he translated to "tortoises don't have feathers, and apples aren't pears". Basically, it warns of a mistruth."

Very quickly the email came back:
OK – sit tight.

Nothing more happened for two whole days.

Leni was beginning to panic and Laurie was becoming unsettled.

"Why hasn't he replied?" Leni asked him when the two were sitting alone in the dining area after the rest of the family had gone to their rooms. They were not a novelty anymore and the family members no longer wanted to engage them in conversation after dinner.

"He is a cop, he doesn't send messages unless he has something to say. The email might be insecure."

"I that why you sent stuff in Afrikaans?"

"Yes – not many people in Indonesia can speak it."

"I didn't know that you can speak it."

"I can't really – I just know a few words and a lot of slang which I picked up, mostly from Johann."

"Why do you think that it is taking so long?"

"Well, either he has dobbed us in to the government, in which case we will have agents come here very soon and we will get shot.

Or, the email has been intercepted and he will get shot also.

Or, he is organizing to get us to Freeport and will let us know when he has done it.

Just then 'Mother' burst in the room.

"I just got a reply from Mr. Johann."

They got up and followed 'Mother' as she ran back to her office.

They both read the email on the screen.

Truck,

Can you get to the M-Regency Hotel in Makassar on Monday?

I can have passes and tickets delivered on Monday night for flight Tuesday AM.

I have registered you at the hotel in your name only. I will leave it to you to figure out how to get your GF smuggled in without using her passport.

My P.A. Ratna will meet you at Timika and drive you up to meet me. Your security is still current from the last time that you were here. You are here to assist me (And actually, I really can use your advice) Ms Herianto is your P.A.

Please urgently confirm if this is OK?

Safe travels

Johann

Leni and Laurie did a Hi Five and they hugged and kissed 'Mother'. It was Friday night, they had three days to get to Makassar.

Laurie emailed back immediately:

All good – thanks mate!

'Mother' decided to go to bed at this point. "I guess that you two have much to discuss so I will leave you to it. Goodnight."

"Goodnight 'Mother'" they said in unison and then Laurie said thanks for everything."

"What are you going to do to 'figure out' to get me into the hotel, without using my passport?" Leni asked.

Laurie began to speak slowly as he voiced what he was thinking. "Well, I'm not really sure but, unless you want to sleep on the street, I need to get you up to the room somehow. Johann is correct – You mustn't use that passport of yours unless you have to. All hotels are obliged to record who their guests are and that means showing some ID which is usually a passport or an identity card."

He paused for a while before he continued. "I think that I have an idea but it will be a bit demeaning for you – I'm not sure that I should ask you to do it."

"Demeaning sounds better than dead," she whispered, "what are you thinking?"

"Well, almost every hotel in Indonesia supports prostitution in one way or another. Many supply the girls themselves but even if a guest brings one in from outside they can't really stop her coming in with him because the practice, though widespread, is still illegal and they wouldn't want to make a fuss or worse embarrass a paying guest."

"You want me to be a hooker?"

"Well, er yes! – I can't think of any other way."

"OK! I'll do it."

"All right, and I'm sorry – I just can't think of any other way."

"So, what should I do?"

"Well, what if you dress normally to travel on the bus but when you get to Makassar you should change into something that looks like what a hooker would wear. You do know how a hooker dresses?"

"Of course, I have seen lots of them hanging out near the government offices in Jakarta."

"Good, I will leave it to you to decide what to wear. Be sure to get a shoulder bag because hookers always carry a credit card machine and various sex toys in it."

"I can put my travel dress in the shoulder bag when I change out of it."

"Yes – good idea."

"Unless you want me to put some sex toys in the bag." She said laughing.

"That's your call!" he exclaimed joining in her laughter. Secretly, he was happy that she had accepted his proposal.

Secretly, she was thinking that he seemed to know a lot about prostitution. She hoped that this would be the opportunity to change him back to being a one-woman man, her man.

Then they went to bed, each in their nominated room, but it was hard for each of them to sleep.

The family had mixed feelings when they announced on Saturday morning that they would be leaving on Monday. Some, particularly Rachel, urged them to stay. All of them were happy that a way to greater safety and a better future lay ahead for them. Nonetheless, there was a pervading sense of disquiet since all that was in place was a flight and some short-term accommodation at Freeport. Laurie had no specific plans in place after that.

It became a busy weekend with the entire family doing various chores to send the couple on their way. There was no surprise when Rachel volunteered to drive them to the 7-Eleven to buy some necessities for the journey.

Laurie made his bus booking from the small travel agency near the 7-Eleven while 'Mother' booked Leni on line. They felt that it was important not to allow the bookings to be linked. Laurie paid 80,000 Rupiah for his trip while the on-line fare was 75,000Rp.

Chapter 9 – Sad Goodbyes

They left early Monday morning for the drive to Rantepao, which took three hours. There was one large backpack in the boot of the old Toyota Hi Lux. It was full of clothes and food that the family insisted on giving them. Leni was carrying a large leather shoulder bag.

Mother dropped Laurie a couple of streets away from the bus terminal in Jl. Mappanyukki. She stopped the truck and reached over in her seat and kissed him. "You are a lovely man, Truck, may God bless you and keep you safe." There were tears in her eyes,

Laurie replied, "Thank you, Ruth, we are both so grateful to you and your family for all that you have done for us." Then he got out of the car and took the backpack out of the tray and walked off before turning and waving back at the truck.

Minutes later Ruth pulled into a parking bay at the bus terminal. The two women got out and hugged. With tears in her eyes, the older woman said, I love you Leni, my whole family does, you must promise to come back and visit us again."

"I will Mother, I will."

"I want to say something else. I believe that God put you in that plane with Truck. I can see that you two are just right for each other. I know that my daughter went to his bed on the night when we were all drunk from the funeral party but I also know that it didn't mean anything. She is young and driven by her hormones and he is a sad lonely man. Promise me that you will forgive him and love him. He is a good man and I think that he loves you."

Leni was expecting an emotional farewell but this was unexpected. She burst into tears and hugged the older woman tightly.

"You are right Mother," she said, "I will take heed of what you say."

They kissed again before she turned and walked into the terminal.

After about five minutes, Laurie walked in and sat with his back to her.

The very modern, air-conditioned, red and blue "New Liman" bus pulled in. Leni got to the front of the boarding queue. By the time that Laurie boarded, fortunately all the seats were taken in which he could sit by himself. There were a few seats left where he had to sit beside someone. One such seat was beside Leni. So, he sat there. It was hardly likely to arouse suspicion since they had made a point of not knowing each other in the terminal and once in a bus, it was perfectly expected that a tall single Australian travelling alone would sit beside a pretty woman with a vacant seat beside her.

Initially, they said nothing to each other.

As the Eight-hour trip ensued, they did chat to each other as any two passengers would as the spectacularly beautiful scenery came into view. They could not help but enjoy the green mountains, lush paddy fields and waterfalls. The trip took around nine and one half hours including occasional stops for comfort and buying snacks.

The other passengers were made up of tourists and locals who had jobs in Makassar or who had fly in fly out jobs in surrounding mines. With it being such a long trip, there was quite a bit of conversation between seats and Leni said that she was going home to see her mother. She hoped that this would explain her comparatively small travel bag.

When they did eventually get to the Makassar bus terminal, they needed to push through the throng of potential porters, tour guides and possibly a prostitute or two. They were all vociferously offering their services. Laurie sought out a Golden Bird taxi and gave his bag to the driver while Leni discretely climbed in through the street side door. The vehicle was quite hot when they got settled in but the driver turned on the air conditioner and set it to run flat out. Both relaxed into the coolness of the vehicle as they enjoyed the half hour drive to the hotel.

Laurie asked the driver to stop in a shopping centre near the hotel to allow "my girlfriend out to do some shopping".

He watched the beautiful woman walk into the crowd of shoppers. She was obviously wearing the money stuffed nursing bra that her cousin gave her but apart from her abundant bosom, she looked quite conservative in the floral shift that she wore with a white pleated knee length skirt. She was wearing a pair of dainty but flat heeled shoes. His throat constricted in panic as he saw her disappear from view. Now that she was alone where he couldn't care for her would she be OK?

He checked into the hotel. There was a booking for him which had been made by Freeport. He was asked to show his passport which he did and the young receptionist photocopied it. She smiled at him very sweetly when she handed him the key said, "If there is anything you want – Anything at all just call me, OK."

"OK," he replied and declined the assistance of the bellhop to carry his bag and nodded to the security guard who was standing near the lifts. He found the room and used the bathroom before having a shower and dressing in the best of his clothes. He went downstairs and out into the street. He paced up and down for about ten minutes waiting for Leni to appear. He was beginning to panic again when she walked up behind him and asked, "Hello Mister, you want girl tonight?"

He turned around and it was all that he could do not to smile. She was wearing a pink elasticized boob tube that extended from just above her breasts to about two inches above her navel. It had little blue bows at the neckline above each breast. It was obvious that she was still wearing the nursing bra underneath but the straps had been removed. She wore a black thigh length tight fitting denim skirt and black patent leather shoes with six inch heels.

He realized that he had not recognized her as he looked down the street moments earlier. "Yes! I think that I would like a girl tonight," he replied.

As they walked back to the hotel, he asked, "Where did you get that outfit?"

"Have a guess." She replied.

"Rachel?"

"You guessed it." She laughed.

When they got to the hotel, he took her hand and escorted her through the door. The flirty receptionist was still at her desk and she looked at Leni disdainfully. Laurie winked at the security guard as they walked past. He smiled back and studied Leni with a lecherous gaze.

They got the lift to Second floor where Laurie's room was situated and he ushered her into the very large room.

She sat on a divan and he went to the fridge and returned with two half size bottles of wine from the minibar. He unscrewed the caps before handing one to Leni. "Cheers!" He toasted to our future whatever it might bring." They clinked the two bottles before they each had a sip. "Are you happy about this?" Laurie asked as he waved his hands expansively to indicate that he was not just talking about the room but having her in it with him.

"I didn't like walking outside on the street dressed like this and I certainly didn't like being leered at by the security guard downstairs. But being alone with you here, in this room, with you, is what I have always wanted from the moment that you sat next to me in the plane."

"It is just what I have been wanting as well. But why didn't you show any interest in me up in Tana Toraja?"

"Because, it would have been embarrassing in front of the family to open myself to you and have you reject me."

"Why did you think that I would reject you?"

"Because I am just a little Chinese Indonesian girl without much money and you are a big wonderfully handsome man who has travelled the world and who must have dozens of beautiful women wanting to sleep with you."

"That is absolutely not true. Sure, I have had quite a few women in my life but I liked you from the moment that we met. We could have kept it secret from the family. I must be honest and tell you that Rachel came to my bed the night of the funeral party when I was drunk and feeling lonely, but the family had no idea. We could have kept it secret."

"Ha! You want a bet! The whole family knows about that and only this morning, 'Mother' spoke to me about it."

"Really, I had no idea, I am sorry that must have hurt you."

"It's OK, you weren't to know how I was feeling."

He took her in his arms and kissed her. She responded passionately.

They pulled back and readjusted her seating in order to kiss without needing to twist their necks. Then they embraced and kissed again more slowly, more sensuously and culminated in their tongues dancing intimately with each other.

Laurie pulled back and held his arms up and said, "Wait! Let's be civilized and order some food and have something to eat before we do anything else. He again used his hands expressively by waving them over the contours of her body when he said the words, "do anything else".

They examined the menu before choosing a pizza which seemed to be the best choice for a couple who urgently needed to eat but who did not want to spend much time doing it.

They chatted while they waited each happy in the knowledge that this was merely to be a hiatus in what was to be a wonderful night of lovemaking. Laurie told her about the PT Freeport McMorran gold mine so that when she arrived, she would have a reasonable idea of the lay of the land.

The pizza arrived along with another bottle of wine along with two glasses and an ice bucket.

Leni stood and walked to a chair and moved it to a position on the opposite side of the coffee table which was in front of the divan on which the pizza and wine had been positioned. Their eyes met as they looked to each other across the low table and Laurie said "bon appetite".

Leni could have held her legs together and turned side on to the table before reaching over to pick up a wedge of pizza. Otherwise, she could have opened her legs around the curved edge of the table and reach forward. She chose to do the latter as she looked into her soon to be lovers in the face with an alluring grin on her face.

The short skirt was not made for modesty. With the hem under tension from the outward pressure of her open thighs, there was nothing to obstruct the man's view of her inner thighs all the way up to her most intimate parts. He became immediately aware of her lack of underwear.

"I'm sure that you could have bought some new panties at the 7-Eleven before we left if you had wanted to" he said with a big grin.

"I didn't want to," she replied sensuously.

"I'm going to get heartburn in my rush to finish this pizza."

"Don't do that, I will be here for as long as you want me."

They certainly didn't waste any time finishing the pizza before getting naked and into the bed. Leni stroked Laurie's erect and throbbing penis with one hand while she sipped the last glass of the wine. Laurie also had one free hand which he used to gently caress her breasts and to roll her tumescent nipples between his fingers.

"Do you have any condoms in your bag?" he asked. "I think that it is time for me to put one on."

"I'm sorry, I haven't got any. I was too afraid to go to a pharmacy this afternoon."

"Are you on the pill"

"Yes! I was, but I lost my purse in the crash. I haven't taken anything since then."

"Shit!"

"I still want you to fuck me. I love you so much that I am happy to risk having a child; in fact, having a child to you would be wonderful."

"I do so very much want to fuck you! He replied, "but getting you pregnant would be a dumb thing to do with so many uncertainties ahead. Don't get me wrong, I would love to be the father of your child but not right now"

"There are other things that we could try. I know that some girls like taking their man in their throat and others like it up their bum."

"Have you done any of those things?"

"No."

"Then I think that I will just masturbate myself and you can help."

"No."

"Why?"

"Because I want to give you my body." I love you too much to watch you relieve yourself without me being involved."

"You would be involved if you help me to wank off."

"Not enough – I want you inside me."

"How?"

"I'd like you to try to take me up the bum."

"No way, much as I might enjoy it, it will hurt you and besides, we need lots of lubricant."

"I've got lubricant."

"Where did you get that?"

"Rachel."

"I should have known?" he said laughing. "How long have you been planning this?"

"All the way down in the bus if you must know." She replied with a coy sparkle in her eye. "I was kind of hoping that you would just take me normally but I suspected that you might be too careful to do that so I decided to have a backup plan. I was able to flush myself out inside in the bathroom of the shopping centre so I am nice and clean inside for you."

By this time, Laurie was almost trembling with sexual lust and he said, "OK, I am going to enjoy this but I want you to tell me to stop if it hurts too much."

"Look," she said, "I have been sitting on the bus getting as wet as wet can be, just thinking about this. Just do it and only stop if I specifically say, 'Get out of me!' otherwise ignore any sounds that I might make and anything that I might say including 'stop'."

"OK."

She knelt on the bed and folded her arms against the sweetly laundered sheet that covered the mattress and rested her forehead on her arms. Her bottom was elevated, and invitingly positioned for his attention. Laurie opened her bag and found the tube of lube. He hastily penetrated the protective foil on the nozzle with the spear in the cap before liberally coating his index and middle fingers. Her vaginal lips were already quite lubricious and ready for penetration. He thought about abandoning his resolve and accepting their salacious invitation but decided not to.

He rubbed the lube over her tiny crinkled orifice and gently worked it down into the tight sphincter. He repeated the treatment and was eventually able to introduce his index finger and after more iterations of lubrication, rubbing and gentle pushing he was able to introduce both fingers. Leni grunted and moaned during the process but they were sounds of enjoyment and encouragement.

Whether her most intimate organ was relaxing or whether it was the effect of his ministrations, he couldn't tell, but it was getting easier to push his fingers inside. Eventually, he felt that it was time to take things to the next stage.

He rubbed lubricant copiously over his penis before gently positioning the soft glans at her opening and pushed gently.

She moaned quietly and said, "That's nice."

He pushed harder and the natural tension in the hollow muscle was unable to prevent penetration of his highly-lubricated glans. She moaned again, more loudly this time as the concept of being widely stretched was becoming a frightening and already a rather painful reality.

He pushed again and the soft glans continued inside and she was now forced to expand to accept the hard roundness of his corona. Suddenly, the extent of her impalement was all too real and as she experienced the extreme stretching and the fullness, she squealed.

The squeal frightened Laurie and he instinctively began to withdraw.

"Don't stop!" she howled, "Just do it."

So, he did. He pushed himself slowly into her depths while she squealed and wriggled beneath him. The delightful tightness around his member which was rapidly steering him to a climax was being provided at a great cost by the woman whose virginal anal canal was being stretched wider than it had ever been in her life to accommodate him.

It didn't take long for her tightness, her wriggling and her howls to bring him to an intense climax. He ejaculated the huge body of his sperm that had built up in the days before as a result of his unrequited lusting after her. He felt guilty that he had actually enjoyed her pain and that her screams had assisted in hastening his climax.

He withdrew his shrinking member and he was soon lying on his back with Leni leaning over him and cleaning him with a tissue.

Soon he noticed that she was looking into his eyes and she looked like she had something to say but couldn't bring herself to say it. What's up?" He asked.

"I need to cum!" She exclaimed, "I am just so turned on by what we just did."

Laurie immediately set about to help her by thrusting his fingers up into her very lubricous vagina while rubbing her clitoris with his thumb. He alternated between sucking on each turgid nipple and occasionally kissing her on the mouth when he teased her tongue with his own. She was soon screaming just as loudly as she had done minutes ago. Her body convulsed with a series of orgasm that sent waves of delight that seemed to extend from deep within her belly down the full length of her sheath.

They lay together exhausted and eventually drifted into sleep in each other's arms.

Chapter 10 – Travelling to a New Opportunity

After a room service breakfast, Leni left the hotel wearing her 'hooker outfit'. The security guard, a different guy from before, hit on her as she was walking through the foyer and told her that he would call the police and have her charged with prostitution. She knew that he wouldn't do it, in fact, it was more likely that he would just drag her out of sight somewhere to rape and beat her up. So, she negotiated with him and agreed to pay him a bribe of 100,000 Rupiah, about $20, and was able to leave without any fuss. She realised that he and his co-workers would have very likely been extorting every working girl that came down alone. Had she left with Laurie, they would not have been game to try anything, but for a man to walk out in the morning with his nightly prostitute would be unusual.

She went to a Dunkin Donuts about a block away and used the toilet to change into the more conservative outfit that she had worn yesterday on the bus. She bought a coffee and sat at a table near a window to wait for Laurie. The girl at the counter was friendly and smiled at her knowingly. It was not unusual for girls in Indonesia to work tricks as prostitutes during the night and then go and work in an office or simply go back to being a wife and mother during the day. This girl had likely seen many similar quick changes occur during her morning shift in the shop.

At exactly 9:00 am, she saw Laurie walk along the footpath outside and she discretely put down her cup with a 10,000 Rupiah tip for the waitress. She walked outside and met Laurie who was standing on the street corner and pretending to try to decide which way to go.

"Hi Mister" she said laughing as she used the usual greeting that Indonesians use when greeting a European.

He greeted her as" Bu" (Mother) which in the Indonesian language is a very common and respectful term for females. They were joking, of course, because they were acting as if they didn't know each other.

"Have you got them?" she asked anxiously, referring to the plane tickets for their flight to Irian Jaya which Laurie was to collect from the hotel reception that morning.

"Yep!" He replied smiling as he patted his coat pocket.

They went shopping. Each bought suitable clothes to wear whilst on site at the mine and on Laurie's suggestion they each bought a set of robust military style khaki coloured trousers and long sleeved shirt. They also bought a couple of heavy-duty backpacks

"Why do we need these?" Leni asked.

"I'm not real sure how this will work out but I am thinking that if we are going to get out of this country, it might require some hiking."

Leni did not pursue the discussion and concentrated on finding suitable clothes. The military style shirts were not designed for a woman and, even though she bought one that was a bit too large for her with her fingers only just protruding from the ends of the sleeves, the shirt still pulled tightly over her breasts encased as they were in the nursing bra which was still stuffed with cash.

Eventually, after getting some lunch at a restaurant overlooking the beach, they caught a taxi to the airport.

They hung out in the departure lounge and Laurie recognised some other Freeport staff and contractors whom he had previously met. In some cases, he shook hands with them and on two occasions, he introduced Leni to them as his assistant.

It required an act of will for both of them to get back on a plane so soon after their recent experience.

Leni took Laurie's hand and squeezed it firmly as they took off.

"Are you scared?" he asked."

"Yes! But not as much as I was after I left you this morning."

"What happened this morning?"

"The security guard hit on me and extorted 100,000 Rupiah."

"Shit!" Laurie exclaimed. "I should have thought of that. What happened?"

"He said that he would call the cops but I knew that he wouldn't do that but it was likely that he would have dragged me into a room somewhere and raped me."

"Jesus Leni, I'm so sorry."

"Don't worry, you didn't think of it and nor did I until it happened. It is easy to forget the risks that prostitutes face in Indonesia."

"It is worse when you think that most of them get forced into doing it. It is seldom a career choice."

They relaxed as best that they could for the remaining ninety minutes of flight time.

They arrived at Timika. It is a small village on the southern coast of Irian Jaya. It provides the shipping and airport services to the massive PT Freeport McMorran mining operation. All of the passengers were made to disembark into a large elevated cage along with all of their luggage. There were dozens of people milling around outside the cage each of whom was intent in spotting the passenger(s) for whom they were waiting. There was a large very full dusty carpark behind the waiting throng. The many vehicles parked there were almost entirely Toyota HiLux.

The security guards laboriously checked each passenger's boarding pass against the tag attached to each item of luggage before the passenger was allowed to exit the cage with his or her luggage. It was a tedious process made worse by the burning hot sun.

Laurie recognized Ratna. The beautiful Javanese woman was standing back and quietly observing the activity going on before her. Laurie waved to her and she nodded and smiled at him warmly. When eventually, they got out of the cage, Laurie introduced the two women each to the other. As Ratna escorted them to her HiLux, she chatted to Leni in high-speed Bahasa Indonesian language that Laurie had difficulty following. He observed then as he had done many times before that Indonesian women speak faster than do the men.

Ratna told Laurie of the changes and events that had occurred on site since his last visit. She updated him with lots of company gossip as she drove them from the port town of Timika along the winding road that ran up through the increasingly dense jungle. They arrived at Freeport company's administrative center of Kuala Kencana (pronounced as Quala Kenchana).

KK as the locals refer to it is a company owned town consisting of housing and facilities for staff. It consists of a couple of large administrative buildings, a shopping center and a couple of restaurants. The houses for the married permanent expatriate staff were quite exceptional. Many had pillars out front and elaborate porticos that would be more in keeping with upper class areas in the likes of Dallas Texas rather than out in the jungle of Indonesia. It was also remarkable in that the edge of the town was very clearly defined. The lush green mown lawn ran to the jungle edge from which a wall of tall trees with interwoven vines ran straight up at that point. Leni noticed during her stay there that butterflies, often large blue ones with wings each the size of a human hand would, occasionally, inadvertently fly out of the jungle wall and then flutter about for a while, no doubt confused, before finding their way back into their habitat.

Their first port of call on arriving in the town was the Golf Course restaurant. Ratna described the golf

86

course as "a wonderful 18-hole facility" and as Leni was later to discover, this was indeed true. She escorted them to a table where a man was sitting looking at his laptop.

The big barrel chested Afrikaner stood up and gave a robust man hug to Laurie and asked, "Haai Truck! How are you mate?"

"Good dankie," he replied. Then they engaged in the chit chat and happy banter of two old friends meeting. When this had subsided, Laurie introduced Leni. Johanne shook her hand very respectfully and, speaking in perfect accent free Bahasa Indonesian, welcomed her and said that he hoped that she would have a pleasant stay at Freeport.

They sat at the table and made small talk before Johann told them that he had got them a house in the town as a result of one of his staff who was on maternity leave and who would be happy for someone to house sit for her. He said this while looking at Ratna who was nodding her head which made it clear that she was the one who had really organized this.

As she listened to this jovial man, she thought of Laurie's description of him "as a great guy and a linguistic genius who can speak many languages fluently except English which he destroys not only with his Afrikaans accent but to make matters worse, he drops Afrikaans words into English sentences."

Eventually, after the demolition of two stubbies each of Australian Fourex beer by the men and one glass each of chardonnay by the women, Johann said, "OK Leni, I know all about this guy," he said pointing at Laurie. "But tell me all about yourself and why the government is so angry at you that they crashed a fucking plane to get at you?"

"How did you know that?" she asked shocked.

"We had heard," looking at Ratna to include her in the conversation, "that the government had shot down a plane and that they are doing a pretty good job of hiding it. From your reaction, you were on it. Ja!"

"Yes, that's how I met Laurie. We were the only survivors. But how did you know about the crash?"

The joviality faded from his face and he looked at her eye to eye and clearly gave the message that only he would ask questions. Then he smiled reassuringly and said, "Now tell me everything. Where were, you born?"

So, she told her story but left out her meeting with Joyce because she didn't want to involve her.

When she finished, she looked at Johann and smiled.

He did not smile back. "Miss Hong, the passport that you carry is in the name Joyce Herianto. Mrs Herianto is a mother currently living in Jakarta. She is you cousin. Did she lend you her passport?" he asked.

"Yes." She replied. "I'm sorry."

"Dis OK. You love your cousin and you didn't want to involve her. But, when I say tell me everything, I mean everything."

"I will, I'm sorry"

Ratna put her hand on Leni's wrist and said reassuringly, "Mr De Kock knows everything. He gets information from all over the country. He is a good man and he will help you but do not ever try to keep anything from him. She looked at her boss with an expression of deep respect bordering on love.

"Lekker!" The big man expounded. "Ratna, can you take Leni back to the house and get her settled in. I need to discuss some business with Laurie."

So, the two women departed.

"What does 'Lekker' mean?" Leni asked Ratna as they walked out.

"Anything that is good or better in Afrikaans," she replied. "You learn a lot of African words if you hang about with him – some you need to be careful not to repeat." They both laughed.

Johann ordered two glasses with a double nip of Glenfiddich single malt whisky.

"Gesondheid!" he said raising his glass. Laurie raised his and tapped the two together before saying "and friendship".

The two old friends discussed Leni's situation and Johann remarked that he felt that it might be possible to get her to Australia via Papua New Guinea. "People have crossed the border from here into PNG before. The locals do it quite often but they have lived here since time began. The border means nothing to them" He said.

"Do   you   know   how   it   is   done?"

"No, but I will find out."

"I need to explain my official position to you," Johann said very formally.

"OK?"

"I need to do what is in the best interest of my employer and that includes ensuring that the company is not in breach of Government legislation. By bringing you on site, I am sure that you will greatly assist the company as you have done before. I understand that Miss Hong, your assistant, is competent and I have checked the records of her previous employer and they say that she resigned. Her name is not on the official lists of people wanted by the police or any other government agency. She is travelling under the name Joyce Herianto. There is no law that says that a person cannot use a different name as long as she does not use this to defraud. There is no indication of any fraud with this woman. She claims that she is using this other name because she believes that government operatives are after her. She talks of being in a plane crash and that she believes that it was shot down. I have received no official notification of any sort of a crash, deliberate or otherwise. I can only conclude that she has some sort of paranoid delusion…"

"But I was in the …" Laurie tried to interject.

Johann help up his hand. "I do not know of any crash," he continued speaking very firmly. "and, I must to say that if I threw everybody off site who is delusional then many staff, probably including myself, would all have to go." He smiled.

"It would make no difference to me if Leni called herself the Virgin Mary, as long as she does a good job and does not endanger the security of the operation."

He paused before saying. "That is my official position, do I make myself clear?"

"Perfectly – thanks mate."

"There is something else that you need to know."

"What's that?"

Well, you know that things have been bad in East Timor since 1975 when Indonesia invaded them."

"Yep! And Whitlam, the Australian Prime Minister encouraged them."

"Indeed! well, the UN has given the Timorese a vote and they voted overwhelmingly to become independent   from   Indonesia."

"I heard that a vote was going to happen but I didn't know that it had happened already or that there was a win for the separatists. So, what happens now?"

"Well now, the shit has hit the fan. Indonesia is sending in militia…"

"You   mean   soldiers   who   aren't   wearing uniforms!"

"Exactly   and   they   are   stopping   a   new administration being formed."

"Sounds bad."

"It gets worse, your Aussie Prime Minister, Howard, is not going to let this happen and he is planning to send forces into East Timor and,… and this is why I am telling you this, Australia could be at war with Indonesia."

"Oh shit!"

"Yes, and you my friend and all the other Aussies on this island would be enemies of the country and would likely be taken into custody."

"How does this effect my current situation?"

"It doesn't – but you're staying here might come to a rapid end if things go badly. Also, you might encounter some antagonism from some of the Indonesian employees – especially the Moslem ones."

Then they discussed the matter that required Laurie's specialist knowledge of corporate software. They had discovered a fraud being perpetrated by a woman in Human Resources which was only uncovered through a lucky accident. What they needed was to create some safeguards built into the software and the data entry process to flag such frauds from these data when it was entered into the system. A meeting had been called for Wednesday, two days away, and Johann wanted to know if Laurie would be able to attend. Laurie was, of course, quite willing.

Over another round of single malt, the two friends got down to discussing some much more serious business namely, the Rugby World cup.

Johann signaled to a waiter and minutes later a driver appeared who took Laurie to his assigned house.

Leni rushed to him and with arms outstretched hugged him. She described how she and Ratna had been talking and Ratna had suggested that the best thing that she thought that they should do would be to hike across the border to Papua New Guinea. Laurie laughed to himself. Obviously, Johann and Ratna had discussed Leni's situation well before they had arrived. He wondered just how much of Leni's story he already knew before he had asked her to tell it.

Next Leni picked up a small blister pack of tablets and waved them to him. He could see that one tablet was missing.

"Ta Daa!" she exclaimed.

"What's that?" He asked.

"The pill. Ratna says that women can buy them at the pharmacy here in KK without a prescription and without a passport. She gave me this monthly pack of hers which I will replace for her tomorrow."

"That's great! How soon does it take for them to work after you start taking them?"

"That is the really cool thing! If you start taking them within five days of your period, you get protected right away."

"When was your period?"

"Four days ago,"

Laurie smiled.

Chapter 11 – A Trek to Freedom

Ratna picked the couple up from their allocated house at 10:00am the following day.

Laurie had been woken earlier that morning with Leni coaxing his flaccid penis to life by taking it in her mouth.

Her efforts were soon rewarded and she was soon straddling him with his member deep within her.

Laurie had enjoyed the bodies of many women during his life but none had displayed the ability to control her kegel muscles like Leni could do. They were both gasping and moaning with delight as Laurie surged to a powerful orgasm while Leni continued to experience waves of delight even as Laurie's member began to soften.

As they lay together Laurie commented on her muscular control.

"My mother taught me that if a woman makes her man happy, he will do the same for her."

"Your mother was a wise woman, where did she get it from?"

"Her mother. All the women in my family are taught the exercises as soon as they start to bleed. My cousin, Joyce, does it too – of course. It is a tradition in our family that goes all the way back to when my ancestors were still living in China."

"It is remarkable that your family has endured for such a long time."

"We always have lots of children."

"Gee! – I wonder why?" joked Laurie.

"I am so happy that you found the pills so fast, I wouldn't ever want to take you like I did in Makassar."

"Why? Didn't you enjoy it?"

"Yes, I did very much, but it hurt you."

"Not all hurt is bad. Women have babies and do all sorts of painful things to make their men happy. My mother still lets my father take her there on special occasions."

"What sort of occasions?"

"Father's birthday, Christmas and Chinese New Year."

"Your mother is a very special lady."

"She is Chinese."

"Says it all, I guess."

They got out of bed, showered and ratted around the pantries and located a box of Korn Flakes. The milk in the fridge was unopened and fresh and they could make coffee. They were dressed and ready by 10:00Am.

As they stood outside the front door waiting for Ratna to arrive, Leni asked, "Do you think Johann is bonking Ratna?"

"Probably, Johann is not into celibacy and she is beautiful and she is smart."

The conversation came to an end when the lady in question drove up in her Hilux.

They climbed in and exchanged "Pagi"s (good morning).

"Did you sleep well?" Ratna asked with a suggestive giggle.

"We did sleep very well and we put your tablets to good use," Laurie replied while Leni looked at the floor very coyly.

"Too much information," the Javanese beauty replied laughing happily.

They spent the day getting settled into the company with ID tags, Laptop and offices.

They were looked after by Grace Wong. Another Indonesian of Chinese descent. She was round faced with a slim build and was an honours graduate of the University of Jakarta. She wore a pair of glasses with circular black rims. Her face bore the marks of what appeared to be a case of severe acne earlier in her life. She was an extremely clever young woman who seemed

94

to have a very detailed understanding of all of the operations on site as well as a very close grip of the operation of the Corporate IT System and she discussed this in minute detail with Laurie.

In the course of introductions, they again met Joshua from Tana Toraja. They talked of his family and Joshua told them that his mother had instructed him to "look after you guys."

"We love your family very much," Leni remarked with tears in her eyes. "I do hope that we will get to see them again."

Grace took them for a drive around KK and showed them the Olympic sized Swimming Pool, the cinema, a more detailed look at the golf course and the restaurants. After this, the 3pm shower began. Because of its geographic location, this region has rain almost every day during the wet season. The rain almost always begins around 3pm and is usually over by 5pm. She dropped them off at 4pm at the shopping centre where they wandered about buying food and other necessities. Leni went to the pharmacy. They got a taxi back to their house.

Ratna picked them up at 8am the next morning and took them to their offices which were not very far from hers. Laurie was given a private office closed in with glass walls and Leni was given a desk in a nearby open plan area which she shared with four other women and a nice guy named Bambang.

The meeting began in a conference room nearby. Present were Johann, Ratna, Grace Wong, the personnel manager, an Australian guy named Pat Sampson, along with Laurie and Leni.

It became quite obvious early in the meeting that all Sampson wanted to do was claim that the woman who had stolen the funds was no good and that there was absolutely nothing wrong in his department. The discussion proceeded with Laurie and Johann looking to identify measures that would provide lasting protocols that would make the perpetration of such a fraud more obvious in the future. Laurie asked Sampson quite a few questions. Many were phrased along the lines, "I'm confused, can you please explain to me ..."

Laurie had long ago learnt that in business, it is often better to feign confusion rather than disagree.

The meeting continued with the discussion raging between the three expatriates. Then Laurie used a skill that more than anything else had made him successful in working in Indonesia.

"What do you think, Grace?" he asked. "What are the issues that you see that make us vulnerable to future fraud?"

He was not surprised when the young woman, whose culture made it very difficult for her to interrupt a conversation between strong minded white men, smiled at him for this courtesy. She then succinctly summarised the points that had been made previously and then counting off on the fingers of her hand listed the five areas of vulnerability that the department faced and which needed to be addressed. She then adroitly inferred that all these points that she had listed had really been what Mr Sampson had earlier suggested.

"Absolutely!" said Sampson puffing out his chest.

The meeting finished soon after that with Laurie saying that "He and Leni will prepare a series of suggested system changes that Pat's team had identified." He then suggested that Leni and Grace should schedule regular project meetings.

The meeting concluded amicably with Sampson feeling that he had won the day.

"What a dick!" said Johann to Laurie. "I'm sorry that you have to put up with that."

"I thought that you were very clever to ask Grace's opinion." Leni confided.

Later Laurie called Leni into his office after he had listed a series of system related matters where he need to know how Human Resources handled them.

"Can you call Grace and discuss these points with her." He handed her his phone.

He watched amused as his lover called her new friend and suddenly exploded into a lengthy discussion "Ta ta tata tat "of rapid Bahasa that he could only barely understand. Suddenly she said "Terima Kasih." (thank you) and hung up.

"I'll do up a document of what she told me." Leni replied.

"In English."

"Sure," she replied not understanding why he was grinning.

He was grinning because he had seen many previous examples where these clever Indonesian women work with each other always communicating in this rapid-fire Bahasa and with friendships that ignore organisational barriers. The conversation always finishes with "Terima Kasih"

The girls all went to dinner that evening at the Chinese restaurant while Laurie and Johann ate at the golf club after a late afternoon game.

"I've been asking if it is possible to get to Australia by trekking into PNG." Johann remarked after they finished desert and were starting on the first single malt.

"What did you discover?"

"Well, it does seem like it might be possible to hike across the border from a place called Oksibil in Irian Jaya to Tabubil in PNG which is where BHP Billiton's OK Tedi mine is located. But it would be bloody dangerous"

"Yep, I've been to Ok Tedi. Leni is determined to have a go at this. I guess when the government shoots you out of the sky, you can be excused for becoming a bit paranoid. I will go with her on this and try to make sure that she doesn't get killed in the attempt."

"As I see it, once you get Leni out of this country without letting the government see her on the way out, you should be OK. If you guys can get across the border to Tabubil, you should be able to get a flight to Pt Moresby without any trouble. Getting from Moresby into Australia will be difficult though."

"I have spent a lot of time in Moresby. I know of a guy who flies regularly from Moresby to Melbourne. He will do a touch and go at a bush airstrip along the way. People that I know have got him to drop off pets at this landing strip rather than go through the extensive Australian quarantine. Maybe, he will drop off a person if I pay him enough."

"If you threaten to expose his pet trafficking it might make him more willing to co-operate."

"Still, I'm not happy about committing Leni into the hands of a shyster like that."

"Maybe, you could just get a boat and head south through the Torres Strait islands. If you get picked up by the Aussie Customs guys or if you make it to the mainland, Leni can then claim asylum seeker status at that time."

"The whole plan is risky and could come unstuck in many places. I'm still not sure that I want to try it?"

"Leni is a remarkable and very determined woman."

"Well, she can't stay here at KK forever. Sooner or later, we've got to try to escape this country."

"OK, I will see what I can come up with."

"Thanks mate – I appreciate it."

"Nie te dankie" (Your welcome).

They continued to work at Freeport and Johann was very happy with the protocols and system changes that they made to the HR system.

Meanwhile, as a background activity, they were planning what they called "Operation Escape". They both worked on the project but Leni especially put a lot of work into it. They ordered equipment and downloaded many images from Google earth. Their trek was going to be formidable in the mountainous and densely wooded country. They would claim to be amateur biologists who were searching for new species of snail. They would have sample bags and would give every indication that they were going on a field trip. There were a few settlements and bush tracks which they would pass through where they would go snail chasing to reinforce their cover story. The route that they choose was certainly not the straightest but avoided as much as possible the dense jungle and steep slopes. The 73kM straight line route would be well over 100kM because of the detours required.

They were able to buy quite a good quality compass from the trade store in the town and Laurie purchased a GPS on Amazon.

They felt that they needed some protection and Laurie discussed with Johann where they might be able to purchase some weapons. Johann replied that he was absolutely unable to supply weapons to any civilian on site. Then he said, "You might keep your eyes out, there are a lot of military around and they can often be careless about what they leave lying about."

It seemed a strange thing to say and he wondered if he meant for him to find a soldier, which wouldn't be hard since they hung out at the bar quite regularly, and try to bribe him for his weapon. He discussed this with Leni and they both figured that it would probably be safer to hike without a weapon than to try to get one from a soldier.

On the second morning after the discussion with Johann, they walked out the door of their house and lying on the pathway near the front door were three boxes. Two of the boxes each held a Pindad P1 the local copy of the 9mm Browning Hi Power semi-automatic pistol. Each of the 13 round magazines were fully loaded and the third box contained a further fifty rounds of ammunition.

As they carried the boxes back into the house, Laurie laughed and remarked, "It's amazing what you find lying about"

He met Johann later in the day and simply said, "Thanks Mate!"

"For what?" he replied laughing and walked away – obviously not wanting to continue the discussion.

Laurie caught up with Johann. "There is something else that I need to ask of you."

"What?"

Can you ask Ratna to arrange for a scholarship with the Medical Faculty University of Indonesia. There is a young woman in Tana Toraja who is the daughter of the family who rescued us that wants to be a doctor and being the youngest, the family can't afford to send her to uni.

"Why don't you do it yourself?" the Afrikaner asked.

"Because I don't know what might happen with this attempt to get to Tabubil. I would like to know that this lass is being looked after even if the worst was to happen to us."

Later Ratna called Laurie to meet with her in her office. She undertook to make the arrangements and Laurie gave her Naomi's contact details and his password so that she could access his account at Bank Lippo and withdraw the funds needed to set up the scholarship. They also set up another account for Naomi's living costs while she was studying in Jakarta.

"You are a good man, Truck!" she said quietly

"The least that I can do." He replied.

Laurie and Leni made a booking at a guest house in Oksibil for ten night's accommodation and they booked a return flight to Oksibil from Timika. They wanted the people in the small town to think that they were planning to return. Apart from keeping up the pretence of merely being amateur biologists, they were not sure if they would actually be able to penetrate the jungle and they figured that having a return flight booked might be a good back up plan that they, hoped would not be needed.

The flight from Timika to Oksibil in the ATR42-300 twin turboprop aircraft was short but the landing was not for the faint hearted. The aircraft taxied to the small orange brick terminal building with its bright blue roof. Numerous locals turned out to meet the aircraft and many were dressed in their traditional costumes of grass skirts. "Arse Grass'" as Laurie described it from the common vernacular of PNG Pidgin language. For a fee, most were happy to pose to tourists for photographs. All of the women were bare breasted but this was a normal part of their traditional costume and not for the purpose of getting more photograph tips even though that did happen.

They made their way to the guest house that was located near the airport and for a few Rupiah, they had an escort and people to carry their packs, whether they needed it or not.

Laurie's pack contained most of their provisions while much of Leni's pack was taken up with the small inflatable raft that they would use to cross the rivers. They decided that even if a river could be crossed by wading, they would use a raft to reduce, as much as possible, the risk of being taken by a crocodile.

The guest house was clean and comfortable and the lady who ran it and her staff, which consisted of her two daughters, were very accommodating.

They had an early breakfast of nasi goring (fried rice) before they set out. They trekked down the road to the south to a point where, from Google Earth, they could see that the first river was near the road and that there were rocks in the river at that point which formed some mild rapids. It appeared that they could be walked over.

They were right, or at least Google Earth was, and although the rocks were rather slippery and the river was running quite fast, they crossed this first river slowly and cautiously but without incident. On Laurie's suggestion, they tied a rope to join each other's belts so that if one of them slipped and fell, the other could hopefully stop them from being washed downstream.

There was a track that extended into the bush from the river crossing but which gradually became more wooded over the further west that they walked.

As the hiking became more difficult and they frequently consulted the wad of printouts that they had made from Google, Laurie was beginning to feel that they were on something of a fool's errand but Leni refused to be daunted by the increasing difficulty and resolutely wanted to push forward.

It took them the rest of the day to get to the second river. They were both exhausted. Leni cried when she saw the river and realised that crossing it would be difficult and dangerous.

In the failing light, they decided to wait until sun up the next day before attempting the river crossing. They each took advantage of the stop to relieve their bladder and bowels. A sense of privacy caused each to walk out of sight of the other. Removing his trousers, Laurie urinated against a tree and stood wide legged to defecate. Leni, pulled down her pants and squatted as required by her physiology and did what nature required. She paid no attention to the long strands of grass which tickled her most intimate parts.

Later, she rummaged in Laurie's pack and took out a bundle of slightly squashed corned beef and pickles sandwiches, two oranges and two fruit poppers. They sat and chatted and admired their beautiful surroundings. Leni talked enthusiastically about how lovely it will be when they get to Australia.

As the sun set, Laurie told Leni to keep watch while he set about to sleep. He did not find it difficult and awoke at 9pm when the alarm on his watch began to beep. Leni was dutifully still awake but she had clearly been struggling to remain so. He sat awake until 3am watching the stars and listening to the sounds of the jungle. He then gently shook the woman awake and they again changed shifts. He awoke as the sun filtered through the leaves just before 5am and Leni smiled at him.

He attached the billy can to a rope and threw it into the river and pulled it in by hanging the rope over a branch that hung out over the water. This enabled him to lift the can out of the river vertically and not spill much water. She had lit their small camp stove and was ready to put the can on it as soon as he brought it to her. She also had a couple of tea bags ready which she put in the can once it had boiled. She then opened one of the tubes of Carnation Condensed Milk and squeezed a small quantity into the blackness of the liquid turning it a brown colour. They waited for a time and allowed it to cool before they passed the can back and forward to each other each sipping the sweet tea while they ate a couple of muesli bar from their travel pack.

Laurie was unpacking the raft from Leni's backpack when he saw her looking at him in a rather uncomfortable way.

"Are you OK?" He asked.

"I think so but I have a bit of a problem," she replied coyly.

"I have something itching between my legs, I think that it might be a tick."

"It might just be an ant or a beetle – But do you want me to check you out?"

"Yes please," she replied even more coyly.

They had discussed the risk of ticks and Laurie had ordered and packed a small can of Medi Freeze Skin tag remover for inclusion in their meagre firs aid kit.

He motioned to the still uninflated raft spread on the ground and said, "OK my love, get your pants down and kneel up on that so that I can check you out."

She did as he instructed and despite the weird feeling of having to present herself to her man like this in the middle of the jungle, what dominated her thoughts was that he had called her "my love."

She knelt on the thick vinyl and folded her arms against the strongly smelling material and rested her forehead on her arms. She drew her knees up to her belly and presented her bottom for his attention.

Laurie knelt behind her and enjoyed the erotic sight and the scent of her feminine muskiness.

She was aware of his fingers moving in her most intimate places before hearing him say, "you're right it is a tick. The little bugga is burrowing in just between your left labium and your thigh."

"Yep!" she replied, with her voice a little muffled as she spoke to the vinyl. "That's where I cab feel it."

"I'm going to have to spray him now. Are you ready?"

"OK!"

He positioned the nozzle close to the tiny creature and squirted the Dimethyl Ether at it.

Leni squealed as the freezing spray contacted her most sensitive skin but she was careful not to flinch away.

It took only a couple of seconds for the tiny little monster to turn white and die. Laurie brushed it away from her skin and it fell onto the vinyl. He picked it up and noted that it was intact. The head was still very firmly attached to its body which is very important since it is the head which if left in the body will cause paralysis and sometimes death.

Of course, she was unable to see what he was doing and she asked, "What are you doing, did you get it?"

"Yes, I did, I was just admiring the view and remembering how nice it was last time that you were in this position."

"You can do me again if you like."

"Nice thought, but I think that I will take a rain check on that until I get you safely out of this bloody jungle. What I am more worried about is how that fucking tick got through your clothes to burrow in where it did."

Laurie opened a small tube of antiseptic cream and rubbed some on the area where the spray had contacted her skin. Then he playfully smacked her on the butt and said that he was done.

As she was pulling her pants back up, she said, "I think I know how the tick got on me."

"How?"

"When I was having a pee last night, the grass was touching me."

"That would do it. These little buggas can climb up grass as well as fall from trees. You had better get used to pissing like a boy for the rest of this trip."

She poked her tongue at him but smiled.

The inflatable raft that they bought was not big enough for both of them to ride in with their packs. They had chosen the smaller model in order to keep the weight and size that they would need to carry to a minimum. His plan was that Leni would paddle across the river by herself with her pack which would be fairly light since it no longer had a boat in it. He had bought two reels of 4mM x 100M super lite dinghy line which had a 300KG break force.

He connected the small foot operated pump to the dinghy and began pumping. Even though the dinghy was small, it took quite a while to inflate it with the small light weight pump. Leni detached the two halves of the paddle from each side of her pack and screwed them together.

He gave Leni one roll of line which she placed on the floor of the dinghy and he tied the end of the other line to a ring on the rear. They scanned the smooth but fast flowing water for any ripples that might indicate the presence of a crocodile before placing the dinghy in the water and Leni swiftly hopped in and started paddling strongly towards the other side. Her pistol was on the floor between her legs where it would be immediately available should she see a crocodile.

As she paddled away from the river's edge, Laurie played out the line behind her. She made it safely to the far side where she hastily disembarked from the small vessel. The flow of the river had resulted in her landing approximately fifty metres downstream from where she had started. She could have reduced this by paddling against the stream but they had decided to spend as little time on the water as possible and so she had paddled straight ahead and not worry about her sideways travel.

She tied the line to a ring at the bow of the boat and proceeded to use this to tow it upstream. She was able to gain about 20metres by doing this but some low hanging branches made it impossible to tow it any further without stepping into the water. She removed her pack and gun from the raft and waved to Laurie.

He pulled on his line and rewound it back on its spool as he drew the boat back across the river while Leni fed out her line from where she stood.

He placed his pack in the boat and positioned his gun between his feet and quickly clambered in and began paddling as fast as he could. He did not get swept as far downstream as Leni had done not only because he was paddling more strongly but because Leni was pulling on the line as hard as she could.

They both felt quite elated at the success of their river crossing with the tiny inflatable. It took quite some time to completely deflate it and roll it up to be stashed back in Leni's pack.

Their elation soon vanished as they realized how much denser was the jungle on that side of the river. They spent most of the day hacking their way through the densely packed and vine laden vegetation.

They hiked south east towards a clearing that Google Earth had identified as being available and where they hoped that they could make camp. It was deeply frustrating to have spent so much time and effort in travelling such a short distance. By the time that they reached the clearing, both were exhausted and Leni was sobbing as she realized how difficult that their goal of reaching Tabubil would be.

At first, they just collapsed on the ground and lay flat to regain their breath. There were a number of places in the clearing where fires had previously been lit along with items of human refuse that bore clear evidence of previous use. Laurie shot a goanna and cut off and skinned the tail before cutting the pale pink flesh into cubes. They put these into their billy can and poured in half of their remaining water. Leni found some plants growing around the clearing that she remembered seeing people selling at a local market as food. She diced up one of the succulent striped shoots after tasting it and decided that it would add some flavor. It was many years later that she discovered that the name of the plant was "highland pit pit". They had brought a small selection of condiments with them and she sprinkled some of these into the billy as well. They were quite happy with the smell that wafted from their improvised stew. They sat and rested and ate a couple of their museli bars as they waited for the meal to cook on the small camp stove. Before leaving on this quest, they had agreed that they should supplement their rations with some natural protein and from the moment that Laurie had seen the goanna, they knew that this would be the time.

They sat around the billy and took turns in scooping out the food with the swiss army knives, which had a combined fork and spoon tool, that they each carried. Allowing for the fact that there is no better spice than hunger they both found the meal very enjoyable. They later took care of their ablutions with Leni being more careful this time not to make herself vulnerable to ticks.

It was late afternoon when they were lying together propped up against Laurie's pack and relaxing and looking at their maps and google printouts as they discussed how they might proceed on their journey. The billy had again been placed on the stove and the water was coming to the boil. Leni had a couple of tea bags and the condensed milk handy to make tea. They discussed whether it was wise to use almost all of their remaining water but decided that they should remain hydrated and with the likelihood of rain later in the day, they would be able to collect more water somehow.

Suddenly, three men burst into the clearing and ran towards them. They were shouting angrily and one was waving a machete while each of the other two had knives. Leni froze in fear while Laurie scrambled for his gun. He was too slow and all that he succeeded in doing was to identify to one of the men where it was.

In the scuffle the man grabbed the gun and held it to the couple. Laurie was pulled to his feet. While one held his gun on him, the other two pulled open their packs and laughed gleefully as they pulled out the contents. Clearly, the items represented a treasure trove of goodies to these primitive men. Each had a mouth that was dark red with saliva deeply infused with the effect of chewing betel nut.

The guy with the machete indicated that he was going to swing it at Laurie and cut off his head. Leni reached out and grabbed the camping stove, still with the water boiling on it and flung the whole thing at the man. The billy hit him on the back of his head and scalding water ran down the back of his neck and his back. Worse still, the still alight methylated sprits from the stove poured out and soaked into the back of the shorts that he wore and caused even more severe burning. He fell to the ground screaming while one other guy tried ineffectively to assist in beating out the flames.

While the burnt guy lay on his belly screaming, the guy with the gun stood and pointed it at Laurie but the other guy wanted to extract vengeance on Leni for what she had done to his pal. He tore at her shirt in an attempt to pull it off but the thick cotton and the strong buttons resisted his attempt. After repeated tugging, some buttons did eventually come away and some button holes were torn but only the tops of her breasts and her cleavage were visible. He held his knife to her throat and motioned for her to undo the remaining buttons herself which she did. With his free hand, he grabbed the collar of her shirt behind her neck and tore the garment from her body, leaving her naked from the waist.

The native holding the gun on Laurie seemed the junior of the three. He also motioned to Laurie to remove his shirt. Unlike poor Leni, it was clear that all this guy wanted of Laurie, was just the shirt.

This gave Laurie the opportunity to move his body and his hands which acted as a foil to distract the guy from anything that he might do.

Suddenly, Leni screamed as the guy grabbed her left breast and began to twist it cruelly.

Laurie's captor couldn't help himself and he turned his head for just an instant to view the object of his lust.

It is quite difficult to break a person's neck. If he can see what you are about to do, the many strong muscles of the neck along with the cartilage make it very difficult for an attacker to overcome unless the size and strength of the attacker is very much greater than that of the victim. Laurie had been waiting for this guy to turn his head towards Leni so that when he seized the head with one hand on the crown and with the other holding his chin, the muscles would be actually assisting the head to turn. He knew that even so, it would be necessary to turn the head with as much force as he could possibly achieve in order to to break the ligaments and free the atlas vertebrae. Turning the head past that point would be easy. The toothpaste like grey white matter of the spinal cord was then being destroyed by the very bone that nature had designed to protect it.

Laurie looked into the eyes of the man who was now experiencing the last seven seconds of his life. His eyes were wide with an expression of wonderment and fear. His mouth opened and his tongue positioned itself to scream but no breath came from the lungs. The messages from the brain were no longer able to pass through the massive break in the spinal cord.

Laurie seized his gun from the lifeless hands as the man's legs collapsed beneath him and he fell to the ground. The young attacker's last views of his life as he lay face up on the ground were of the clouds in the blue sky above. Seconds later, the effects of hypoxia were to eliminate consciousness and soon thereafter all brain activity ceased.

Laurie took the few steps soundlessly and swiftly to the man who was focused on pulling Leni's trousers down and whose erection left no doubt to his planned next step. He threw him on the ground and kicked him in the buttocks before the lust crazed wretch knew what had hit him.

He motioned for him to stand and he got painfully to his feet. The bruising of his buttocks was obviously causing him great pain. As he stood, he caught sight of his colleague, whom Laurie thought was likely the poor wretches' brother, lying lifeless on the ground.

Laurie put his phone on movie mode and signed to the guy that he wanted him to confess to what he and his partners had tried to do. Whether he failed to understand or was too overcome by fear to speak, was hard to tell. But he looked at Laurie and his mouth remained shut. Laurie pointed to their packs torn open and Leni standing half naked and again pantomimed speaking with his hand to his mouth opening and closing it like the beak of a bird. He then pointed the pistol at the man's scrotum and suddenly he began to talk animatedly in his local dialect. Laurie was satisfied that the guy was telling the story of his attack on them correctly by the man pointing where they had emerged from and the open packs and Leni's nakedness. He paused when he pointed to the young man lying dead on the ground and wailed. Laurie brought this outpouring of grief to an end by moving the gun closer to the man's testicles and made to fire. The native screamed and continued with the story and demonstrated how he had made Leni remove her top and Leni still bare breasted came into the picture. Finally, when Laurie felt that he had got a suitable confession from the guy, he handed the gun to Leni while he took the antiseptic crème from the first aid kit and gently rubbed it onto the worst of the burns on the man who was kneeling on the ground and sobbing. He handed the half empty tube of crème to the companion.

Leni pulled her shirt back on and buttoned it up. She was whimpering from the shock and violence that she had experienced and from the pain in her breast. She knelt on the ground and began replacing the items back in their packs. Laurie with the pistol in one hand and the other pointing to the gap in the jungle from which the three had entered the clearing looked at the miserable pair of men, "fuck off!" he bellowed at them. Whether they understood the words or whether they simply understood his body language, that is exactly what they did. One ran still with tears running down his cheeks from the pain of his burns. The other was totally naked, having left his filthy ragged shorts lying where he had dropped them. The methylated spirits from the stove had burnt out and Laurie waited a while for the stove to cool before he could straighten the metal that had been bent from its having being used as a missile and put it back in the pack.

Once packed, Laurie asked Leni what she wanted to do. They could proceed on with no knowledge of whether the jungle would become more or less dense than what they had already struggled through. He pointed out that their food supply would not last the distance. "Worst of all," he said, "is that we don't know if the three who attacked us have any mates who might want to get even for our killing their brother over there." He pointed at the man lying on the ground with no evidence showing how he died.

Leni began to weep and covered her face in her hands. "I can't do this anymore. I am just so exhausted. Apart from what they wanted to do to me, they would have killed you also. I can't put your life in such danger."

"I don't want you to worry about me, I just want you to be safe."

"Who were those men who attacked us?"

"Well, on the other side of the border, in PNG, they would be called 'raskols'. There are lots of these criminal gangs springing up as law and order breaks down and obviously, the problem is not limited to the eastern end of this island. I don't know what they are called locally, but obviously, they prowl about looking for people to rob and rape whenever they get the opportunity."

"I can't go on!" she cried. "Those men found us and probably others will too. We have to go back."

"Are you sure?"

"Well, I am safe for the moment in the Freeport compound but if the government finds out where I am and they tell Johann to give me up, he will have to do it."

"Well, if it was my call, I think that we have a better chance back at the mine than we do continuing on here. This jungle is bloody thick and only those little robbing bastards know where the tracks are. I think that we are likely to end up dead if we keep going."

"I think so too," she said sniffing back the mucus in her sinuses that was the result of her tears and she began to walk back to where they had entered the clearing.

As she walked close to the young man lying dead on the ground, she stopped and said, "I saw you kill this guy with your bare hands. That was amazing."

"What was amazing is that you had the presence of mind and the courage to throw the stove at his mate. If you hadn't have done that they would have killed me first but you made them mad so they went after you first. Still, the best thing was when you flashed your tits. After that, this guy…" he said looking down at the body. "…didn't have a chance."

"I didn't flash them – they made me do it."

"Even so, it was the best thing to happen all day."

"Men!" she said in mock disgust and hit him playfully on the chest before marching off towards the almost imperceptible gap where they had earlier exited the jungle.

Going back the way that they had come was only marginally easier than hacking through the jungle in the first place. After about an hour, with dusk settling over the jungle, Laurie spotted a large rock which was smooth and free of vines at the top. He decided that it would be the best place for them to stop for the night.

They sipped a small amount of their remaining water and decided on a lookout roster and took turns sleeping. Fortunately, the rock had an indentation in which one could sit and lie back against the rock. They could use their packs to lie against which were softer than the rock but it was a long way from a Sealy Posturepedic, as Laurie joked, but, such as it was, it did provide a relatively comfortable place for an exhausted jungle traveler to get some sleep. The sleeper would rest in the indentation while the guard would squat on the very top of the rock where he, or she, had a 360-degree view around the rock into the moonlit jungle.

Chapter 12 - Failure

Laurie awoke from sleeping, albeit poorly, at first light. Leni was perched above him on the rock having stood guard for the last three hours.

She was weeping quietly. He climbed out of the sleeping niche and gave her a hug before they both kissed.

There was no point asking why she was crying, instead, he said, "Try not let this get the better of you."

"I am just so worried!" she exclaimed.

"Look! We will go back to the mine where you are safe and work out another plan. There is no point worrying!"

"I know what happens to women who get caught by these jihadist military people. They have contacts with people in the mainstream military who hand people like me over to them. They say that we are enemies of the country and these fools believe them. If I get arrested, I will be put in a jail where I will get beaten and raped repeatedly before they will eventually kill me. If they can't arrange for me to get arrested, they will still send a bunch of thugs after me who will be told to rape and torture me before they kill me."

"I know that there are some loathsome extreme jihadists hiding in parts of the military but I have never heard of them being as organized as you say."

"You are not Chinese. You saw what they did all over the country; my mother would have been raped and killed when they looted Glodok Plaza and burnt out the Senen shopping complex. My mother risked being burnt alive in the fire rather than being caught by the looters and the soldiers. Look at the windows of the buildings of Glodok. There were broken windows at floors high above the street. Looters throwing rocks couldn't break them, it was the soldiers with guns who did it."

"OK! I agree, but let's get you back to the mine, there is no point hanging around here. I don't want to meet anymore raskols."

"Maybe those three were sent after us?"

"Maybe, but I don't think so. They were local tribesmen, I don't think that they would co-operate with the government."

They hiked faster through the jungle this time and ditched their little inflatable boat and its pump after making the last river crossing. Leni was close to exhaustion and it was important to preserve her failing energy by reducing the weight that she had to carry.

Leni waved to it as it floated down the fast-flowing river carrying its pump and a few other bits of superfluous luggage, such as the stove and its now empty fuel container. "Goodbye little boat." She said, "You have served us well."

"Yep! she was a good ship." Replied Laurie.

When they made it to the road, they discarded even more superfluous luggage and hiked north to the Oksibil guest house.

They were a day earlier than their booking but that was not a problem as there were no other guests staying there.

The pleasant owner commented on their dishevelled appearance and asked them what had happened.

"We got attacked by raskols." Laurie advised. "They took most of our stuff but we managed to get away."

"They are scum." She replied. "Things are bad enough here without local men going rogue and terrorising people."

She ushered them to the small but clean smelling bedroom which had an adjoining bathroom which was shared with the room next door. Leni was first into the bath while Laurie took the clothes that she had been wearing and tossed them into the washing machine that was down the hall. He returned with her clothes which he had spun dry as much as possible and then placed them on hangers in the bedroom cupboard.

Leni looked at what he had done for her and smiled.

She ushered him to the bathroom and said, "your turn."

As he removed his clothes and tossed them on a seat. she stretched out naked on the bed. They each looked at each other's naked body and smiled as Laurie said, "too tired, maybe later."

When he emerged from a long and luxurious shower and a shave after being able to complete his ablutions in a proper toilet free of ticks and leeches, he saw Leni sitting naked and cross legged on the bed with two large bowls of nasi goring and sets of chopsticks.

"How did you do that? he asked.

"Well, I took your clothes to the washing machine like you did for me"

"Did you put your wet clothes back on?"

"No, because there is nobody else staying here I thought that I would walk down there naked."

"You were very brave."

"Well, yes! but also, very stupid because Bu Nancy, that's the owners name by the way, walked into the hall way just as I was coming back with your clothes. She ignored the fact that I was naked and just asked what I was going to do with your wet clothes and I said that since I had spun them, that I would hang them in our room. She didn't want me to do that and offered to hang them up on the line outside. Then she asked me where my clothes were and I told her that they were already hanging in here. She came here with me and collected my clothes and headed outside with all of our clothes."

"What about the food?"

"Well, that is the really sweet part. Just a couple of minutes ago, she opened the door, she didn't knock by the way, and handed me all this lovely smelling food."

"I'm really getting to like Bu Nancy."

"Me too." She said as she hopped off the bed and passed a bowl to Laurie. They each sat on one of the two chairs and each shoveled the beautiful rice into their mouths while holding a bowl under their chins and very effectively using the chopsticks.

They had finished eating when the door opened again and Bu Nancy burst in seemingly oblivious to their nakedness.

She had two bottles of Bintang beer.

"Breakfast will be in the dining room tomorrow morning. What time do you want it?" She asked.

After looking at each other, Laurie asked if 7am would be OK.

"That will be fine," she replied "You must know that all meals must be eaten in the dining room from now on. I just fed you here, this time, because your clothes were being washed."

"You are most kind, Bu Nancy, we are most grateful," replied Leni.

When they finished eating and had drunk their beer, without saying a word, and despite the fact that it was still midafternoon, Leni pulled back the covers of the bed and they climbed in and were soon enjoying the blissful sleep of the exhausted as they lay in each other's arms.

Much later they were roused as they heard the door open and again Nancy entered. She placed Leni's clothes on one chair and Laurie's on another.

"Thank you." Murmured Leni. As the woman left the room without saying anything.

Leni had turned to lie on her side as she watched the landlady exit the room. She felt Laurie's arms encircle her from behind and his hands cupped her breasts. She giggled as he pulled her back against his hairy chest and she felt his male hardness pressing into her buttocks.

"Do you want my bum?" she asked. She tried to avoid sounding anxious as she said these words because, although she knew that it would be painful to be taken, dry as she was. she was prepared to let this man whom she loved and to whom she was so grateful use her body in whatever way gave him pleasure.

"No lube and not a special occasion," he murmured. "Just lift your knees a bit."

She did as he asked and she soon felt the delightful feeling of the softness of his glans probing gently between her labia which were rapidly lubricating with her feminine juices with each passing second.

She let out a little cry as the hardness of his shaft entered her canal and she felt the most enjoyable small pain as she stretched to accommodate him.

He thrust strongly and soon she felt his mound pressing against her labia as he invaded her to the full depth of his large member. He lay still and enjoyed the squirming movements of the woman now so impaled on him to stimulate him.

Within a short time, she squealed as the beautiful involuntary contractions of her sheath surged delightfully through her belly while her movements caused her man to ejaculate days of pent up sperm deep into her womb.

They lay together and she felt his monster subside to a soft little warm ball of flesh that nestled between the cheeks of her bottom. His hands continued to cup her breasts and she felt the delicious heightened sensitivity verging on a sweet pain as her still turgid nipples squeezed between his fingers.

"I love you!" she said.

"I love you too!" he replied as post coital euphoria eased him back into sleep.

Leni's mind relaxed and for the first time in a long time, she slept soundly.

She awoke the next morning with the sun shining through the window and warming her body. She pulled the blind to block it out. Her movements woke her man who mumbled, "What's going on?"

"This she replied," as she kneeled between his legs and took his member in her mouth. As soon as he was hard, she straddled him and again delighted in being impaled by him. She enjoyed being able to control his orgasm as she bobbed up and down on him leaning forward to allow him to suckle her nipples from time to time.

After they had relaxed, they each had a bath and got dressed. Not only were their clothes washed, they had been ironed and mended as well. New non-matching buttons had been sewed onto Leni's shirt and the button holes repaired where the previous ones had been torn away during the rape.

Leni used her phone to rebook their flight back to Timika that afternoon.

They were greeted warmly by Nancy when they made their way to the dining room.

"Did you sleep well," she asked with a smile on her lips and she put an emphasis on the word sleep. Obviously, she had heard the sounds of their lovemaking.

" Yes, we did sleep very well thank you Bu Nancy," replied Leni also emphasizing the word sleep.

They looked at her in surprise when she asked if they would like bacon and eggs for breakfast. Leni had eaten bacon only once or twice in her life. Laurie had not eaten it since leaving Australia. "Yes please," he replied while looking at her quizzically.

"I am not a Moslem and I enjoy bacon myself. It is easy to buy butchered pig from the locals here and of course the chickens run wild around this village. I assumed that you Mr Australia and you Ms Cina are Christians."

"Yes, we are," replied Leni. She glared at Laurie with a look to say don't say a thing. She did not want to create extra controversy should Laurie mention his atheism.

He got the hint.

She got busy and cooked a mountain of bacon with seven eggs. She sat at the table and loaded her plate. She had two eggs as did Leni while she gave Laurie three eggs.

"Did you find many snails on your trip?" she asked.

"No, "replied Leni, "We left them behind when we ran from the raskols"

"Did they hurt you?"

"No, we were able to run away. They didn't catch us and Laurie fired a gun and they ran off."

"OK!" the old woman said, "I want you to know that I like you and your secrets are safe with me. But I know that what you are telling me is bullshit."

The woman had tears in her eyes as she looked at Leni. "My dear, I know what a woman's blouse looks like after she has been raped. I have seen the bruises on your breasts and they tell what happened to you more clearly than any words that you might say. I know that the only way to escape from those animals who thieve and rape in this area is to kill them if they attack you. I don't want to know what really happened because if you were to admit that you killed anyone then I would be required to report it to the police and I don't think that you would want their attention. Am I right?"

Leni nodded and Laurie glared at her for acknowledging the old woman's assertion.

The old eyes looked at Laurie and she said, "Don't say anything but I believe that you were trying to get across the border to get to Tabubil. I don't think that

122

you, Mr Australia, need to do this because with your passport, you can go anywhere. I think that you are trying to get Ms Cina out of the country and you are a very brave man."

Both guests looked at the old astute woman and tried very hard not to convey any expression.

The old woman laughed. You Miss Cina are being very inscrutable but your frown, Mr Australia, tells me everything. If you want to try again to do this, you must talk to me and I can help you. It is still very dangerous but I can give you information which will help you."

"Thank you, Bu Nancy," said Leni. "That would be wonderful."

"I said nothing," the old woman said with a false laugh, "What wonderful weather we are having and all of my flowers are blooming nicely."

Breakfast continued with pleasant small talk and the old woman like many old mothers seemed to delight in making them eat as much as possible. They told her that they would be catching the afternoon flight and she said that she would refund them for the extra night's accommodation that they had paid for. They would not hear of it.

Her comment about flowers though obviously to change the subject was in fact close to the old woman's heart. After breakfast, she escorted them to her enclosed private garden behind the guesthouse where she proudly showed off her collection of orchids. There was an amazing range of *Dendrobiums* and *Bulbophyllums* but it was the magnificently colored and complexity of the *Rhododendrons* that left Leni wide eyed. even Laurie who was not an anthophile had to admit that the garden was quite spectacular.

Nancy walked with them to the airport and hugged them as they departed. "If you come back, talk to me first."

"We will!" said Leni and they both waved to her as they entered the departure lounge.

The flight back to Timika was uneventful and Ratna met them at Timika airport and escorted them back to Kuala Kencana.

Chapter 13 - Marriage

The next morning Laurie was summoned to Johann's office.

"Your jungle trek was not as successful as you had hoped." The big Afrikaner remarked.

"No, it was very heavy going through the jungle but what really stuffed it up was when we got attacked by raskols." Replied Laurie with deep disenchantment in his voice.

"Yes! Ratna was telling me about that. I want you to write a report about it. You must be totally factual so that I will not get any nasty surprises if I am asked about it by the police."

"Actually, I made a video of the uninjured guy after the event. I tried to make him confess to what they had done but since I don't understand his language, I don't know if what he said is useful."

"Do you have the video with you now?"

"Yes."

"OK, play it."

Laurie took out his phone and played the video.

"You did OK, the *drol* told the story and tried to blame his two brothers for what happened. Everything that he said puts you in the clear as innocent people acting in self-defense and you acted to prevent Leni from being raped."

"He was a little shit – that's for sure." Replied Laurie indicating that he knew sufficient Afrikans to know what Johann had call his attacker.

"How is Leni?"

"She is very shaken by what happened and still in pain from when the little bastard tried to twist her breast off. Most of all, she is very distressed because she hasn't been able to get to Indonesia and away from the Islamists. She is convinced, and so am I for that matter, that as soon as she sets foot off this site they will arrest her and torture and kill her."

"OK, well I can't comment on that but I can say that I am glad that she is OK."

"Thanks"

"Now I do need to ask you something?"

"What?"

"How much do you care for Leni?"

"Very much – she is a fantastic woman and I…"

"OK, OK; Would you be prepared to marry her?"

Laurie paused for a moment and replied, "well yes – if she wants me!"

"Do it!"

"What?"

"Marry her. Things are happening and your being married will help."

"What?"

"I can't say but I can tell you that I am flying to Jakarta tomorrow and I will be away for a week. I am having discussions with the Australian consulate and the US Consulate. I want you to take charge here while I am gone and you need to marry Leni tomorrow if possible. Ratna will arrange the details."

"Maybe I should propose to Leni first."

"That might be a good idea." Replied Johann laughing.

Laurie walked straight to Leni's office.

"Come with me, he asked. "I need to ask you something."

He walked out of the office to Johann's Hilux and Leni followed him and climbed in also.

He drove a short distance to a small recreational park nearby and beckoned her to follow him to a small wooden picnic table amongst the trees."

He sat and Leni sat opposite him.

"What?" she asked.

"Leni Hong, will you marry me."

She looked at him in surprise and said, "shit!"

"You are not supposed to say 'shit' you are supposed to reply 'yes' or 'no'." he said laughing.

"Yes, Yes! Of course, but this is so sudden."

"It is even more sudden – we have to get married tomorrow."

She looked at him with wonderment and again said, "shit."

Laughing loudly, he said, "you are not supposed to say 'shit' you are supposed to say either, 'that will be lovely' or 'get stuffed'."

She laughed and said, "That will be lovely. But why the rush?"

He told her about the meeting with Johann.

"So, you want me to go to Ratna and say, 'Hi Ratna, can you arrange for us to get married tomorrow?'." She asked.

"Yes, but we need to do something else first."

"What?"

"I need to buy you a ring."

So, they drove to the nearby shopping centre and found a store that sold tourist items. To their surprise and delight they found a ring that had 'place of gold' engraved on it and the ring purported to be made of gold although from the price, the gold plating must have either been exceedingly thin or non existent.

When they got back to the office Leni went to visit Ratna to tell her the news. Ratna hugged her and kissed her cheek and congratulated her. Then Leni asked her how she should arrange a wedding in Kuala Kencana and to do it tomorrow.

She was surprised when Ratna told her that the celebrant had already been arranged and the ceremony will be held in the lovely garden behind Johann's house. They had also booked the Golf Club restaurant for twenty guests for a reception tomorrow night. It was obvious that these arrangements had been made at least a day ago. "When did you arrange all this?" Leni asked.

"Yesterday morning, I knew that you two would be getting married before Laurie did."

Leni didn't know whether to be happy or sad at this revelation but simply accepted it without comment.

The wedding it the beautifully cared for garden behind Johann's house was delightful.

The celebrant was a Seventh Day Adventist pastor. He was a very upbeat character who added a lot of humor and goodwill to the occasion. He said a prayer at the end of the service which as expected called on God to bless the marriage and to guide them through the challenges of the future. It was all pretty generic and even Laurie was quite appreciative of the man's efforts to avoid using the occasion as a means to promote his particular faith. The bridal party was made up of Leni who was wearing a white full length dress and with Ratna and Grace as the bridesmaids. Laurie had Johann as the best man and the and the Torajan Joshua as groomsman. There was a Chinese dress designer who operated a dress shop along with a grocery store selling Chinese food. The sweet lady worked all night to modify the two lilac gowns worn by the bridesmaids and the bride's dress. She even managed to provide a pretty silver coated plastic tiara which she attached to a veil which made the bride look very traditional.

Laurie borrowed a suit from Johann which fitted reasonably well.

Leni was amazed when he presented her with a solid gold wedding ring. Inside it was the initials 'A.H.'. "Angela Hudson, my late wife, she would be proud to know that you are wearing it. You can get the initials changed later sometime." He told her.

"I will never change them. It will be lovely to remember her in this way and it will remind me to always try to be as good a wife to you as she was."

A sound squeaked from his throat as he tried to reply but emotion froze his throat and he couldn't speak. For the first time, she saw tears running down the cheeks of her big strong man.

The reception at the golf club went very well. The food was great. And the guests included many from the office, and the dressmaker and her daughter. Johann made a speech which occurred after he had a few single malt whiskeys and some very risqué jokes were included and other references to what was to happen that night after the reception was completed.

Joshua spoke and extended the best wishes of his family to the couple.

Laurie made a speech praising his new wife and declaring how happy she had made him and how he is committed to share her life wherever fate would take them.

Leni did not speak. That was not the sort of thing that a young woman of Chinese descent would do.

After the food was eaten and the speeches made, the guests in what was an Indonesian custom simply stood up, wished the couple goodbye and good wishes and departed. There was none of the extended period of socializing and drinking that was so typical of Western weddings. Laurie expected this because he had attended similar Indonesian weddings before but the nonetheless he did feel a bit cheated on this, his and Leni's special night. Leni, on the other hand, saw nothing unusual having never experienced anything any different.

They did wait until the last guest had departed. Laurie saw Ratna and Leni having a discussion earlier in the evening whereupon Ratna departed hurriedly. Laurie wondered if Leni had said anything that might have offended her but said nothing.

They got back to their house and they found a sealed shopping bag, with a note attached, leaning against the door. The note said, 'have fun, love Ratna'.

Leni smiled and picked up the bag. "What's in there? Laurie asked.

"Oh, nothing," replied his wife coyly.

Laurie shrugged his shoulders before stooping and suddenly picking up his wife and throwing her over his shoulder while clutching her legs to his chest. She was still clutching the bag which she allowed to hang behind his back.

Leni shrieked in surprise, "what are you doing?" she asked.

"Carrying you across the threshold," he said with a tone in his voice in which he expressed surprised that she needed to be told.

"Why? She asked speaking with a high-pitched tone in her voice as a result of her being upside down with her belly pressing down on his shoulder.

"It's a western tradition. Western husbands always carry their new brides over the threshold."

"Why?

"I don't know, it's just a tradition."

"Are there any other weird western traditions that I should know about?"

"No – not that I can think of."

"There might be a problem with this tradition," she said laughing.

"What?"

"Somebody needs to open the door."

It was difficult for him to remove the key from his trouser pocket while carrying the woman over his shoulder but with some wriggling and giggling by both of them, he succeeded and turned the lock and Leni pushed the door open with her foot. He carried her to the bed and dropped her on to it. She laughed but quickly got up from the bed and turned her back to him.

"Unzip me!" she asked.

With her dress hanging from her shoulders, she grasped Ratna's bag and headed for the bathroom. "I

130

might be a while getting ready but please be naked for when I come out."

Laurie did as she had asked and lay naked on his back on the bed with his erection pointing to the ceiling as he anticipated whatever it was that his bride had in store. He heard water running and quite a bit of movement behind the door. The toilet was flushed three times.

She emerged naked while holding something in her hand. "What took so long?" he asked.

"I have cleaned myself inside," she replied "and I have lubricated my bum for you. I want you to enter me as deeply as you can."

She showed him that she was holding a tube of lubricant in her hand.

"This is a special occasion," she said laughing.

Chapter 14 – International Hostilities are Not All Bad

Next morning was a busy time for Laurie as he took over from Johann. Since it was only for a week, it was not as if he would be making policy changes but there were various functions that the security manager was responsible for and Laurie needed the keys to the necessary stores and custody cells in case they were needed and he needed the passwords of the security monitoring systems.

Despite his short time on the site, he was certainly the most experienced security person there and it was logical that he should act for Johann while he was away.

As he drove Johann to the airport, Johann said, "I hope that you enjoyed your wedding ceremony yesterday."

"Yes, I did - thank you," he replied.

"I hope that you didn't mind my pressuring you to move so fast, but you must have realized that I wouldn't have suggested it without good reason."

"Not at all, but I am eager to know what that reason is."

"Of course, you are, and I can tell you that there is certainly something going on but I can't discuss it. When I get back at the end of this week, I probably will be able to.

Laurie went to see Leni in her office when he got back to the administration center to tell her what Johann had said.

He spent most of the week documenting the review of IT security that he and Leni had previously been involved in. He chaired the monthly meeting of the security agents, who were really just spies. Collectively, they were responsible for reporting on events both on the mine site and in the Irian Jaya area. They would each make a report and Ratna would log their comments.

Sometimes action like deploying additional resources to an area would be made but most times, each situation would simply be noted.

He was surprised when an agent reported that a father and his two sons had been attacked in the jungle southeast of Oksibil. The father had been severely burnt and one of the sons had been killed from having had his neck broken. The uninjured son had claimed that they had been attacked by a large group of Javanese people that had been led by an expat. The agent asked the lady who ran the guest house if there had been any expats and Javanese people staying there who said that there had only been a man and a woman who had been there to collect snails.

"How is the burnt guy?" Laurie asked.

"He has been treated and although his back will be badly scarred, he will be OK."

"Are the police following up on this?"

"No, these three were known to be raskols and probably they tried to rob some local tribes people who fought back."

Laurie then moved the discussion to the next item of business.

Johann returned as expected at the end of the week and immediately called Laurie to his office and asked him to give him an update on what had been happening while he had been away. Laurie mentioned the report about the raskols and Johanne looked at him but nodded and said nothing. At the end of the briefing, Johanne phoned Leni and asked her to join the meeting.

As soon as she sat down in his office, Johann began to speak. "I have been speaking to our head office and the site manager and this week, I had a meeting with the Australian High Commissioner in Jakarta. Australia, in conjunction with the United Nations is heading up what is basically an invasion of East Timor with a peacekeeping force to be called INTERFET. The intent is to drive out the Indonesian sponsored militias currently in that country. As a result of the deteriorating situation in East Timor and the ill will that is developing in this country towards Australia, all Australian staff and contractors on site here will be evacuated back to Australia in two weeks' time."

Leni began to cry.

"Leni," he continued, "I told the commissioner that one of my Australian contractors has married a local woman and that she needs to be evacuated as well. I explained that you were facing serious danger in this country and that you also needed to be evacuated. The commissioner explained that the Australian Government had only last month introduced instruments called Temporary Protection Visas where people who are being persecuted in their country could be granted residency in Australia until their status could be assessed. Since you are married to an Australian Citizen, then that will simply be a matter of course. The TPV will allow you to stay in Australia while your marriage visa is being processed."

"So,   I   can   go   to   Australia?"

"You can go to Australia."

Leni ran to Johann and threw her arms around his neck and kissed him.

The next two weeks were hectic. All Australian employees and contractors needed to be contacted and many had employment contracts that were going to be broken. Many wanted to stay but they had to be made to understand that they needed to be evacuated now because if the relationship with Indonesia deteriorates to all-out war then they would be imprisoned. Laurie and Leni along with Ratna and others arranged the evacuation.

During the hurly burly, Ratna took Laurie aside. "I have arranged the medical scholarship for Naomi.

The family is very grateful. A lady named Ruth said that she wishes you and Leni God Speed and that she wants to see you back in Tana Toraja very soon.

Soon after, Joshua visited Laurie in his office. "You didn't need to do that, Truck. Our family enjoyed your visit. We are most grateful for what you have done for Naomi."

The unassuming Laurie felt uncomfortable in the face of such gratitude and simply said, "It is my pleasure, I'm sure that Naomi will become a fine doctor." Then he broke of the meeting by saying, "I'm sorry, Mate, I've got lots of work that must be done."

Joshua shook Laurie's hand with both of his and said, "Good luck, my friend." And he walked away.

The evening came and a convoy of company vehicles delivered the many Australian staff and contractors to the small airport. There were many handshakes and man hugs between the departing Australians and their Indonesian workmates. There were also some tearful embraces and kisses between a few male and female staff whose relationship had clearly developed beyond merely being workmates.

An officious Javanese security guard was checking that all the intending passengers had an Australian passport and that their name was on a list provided by and signed by Johann. He rejected Leni because she did not have an Australian passport and, in fact, she did not have a passport at all. She showed the document provided by the Australian embassy but the guy was an obtuse sort of person and would not accept it. Eventually Laurie rang Johann and handed the phone to the guard after he explained the problem. The guard listened to the site security manager before saying "Yes sir," and stamped her papers.

The departure lounge was really just a wire cage with long forms as seats. There were two gates and a unisex toilet. One gate was open and was manned by the officious and self-important Indonesian guard who had a pistol on his belt and another Indonesian defense force guard who stood beside him and was holding a submachine gun. The other gate which led to the tarmac was locked. The situation was intimidating. After they had been sitting for about forty-five minutes, one contractor asked loudly, "Is this fair dinkum or are we going to get taken prisoner?"

Another replied, "We are already prisoners, we are locked in here with a guy at the gate with a fuckin sub machine gun."

Laurie took control, "Settle down, you blokes, I helped organize this. I don't know why the plane is late but it definitely has been arranged to take us home."

"I fuckin hope so," said another contractor.

Laurie rang Johann again and told him that the plane hadn't arrived yet.

"I know," said the South African, "There is chaos in the Indonesian Air Traffic control because the Australian and United States Air forces are forcing aircraft into what the Indonesians consider to be their sovereign airspace."

Laurie stood and shouted this message to the anxious passengers.

A half hour later a plane could be seen landing. Many eyes peered through the gloom to see what it was.

"A voice shouted out, "It's got the flying kangaroo on the tail, Its fuckin Qantas."

Men from other nations might have cheered at that moment and there were certainly some loud sighs of relief but the laconic Australians simply responded, "shit yeah!" after one of their mates called out "fuckin beauty!"

Laurie again called Johann, "It's here, he told him."

"bakgat!" he replied, "It has been in holding for quite a while and can now only get to Darwin with its remaining fuel. Good luck *boet"*

"Thanks mate, I'll be in touch!"

"Johann said that's cool and told me that the plane has been circling and now has only sufficient fuel to get to Darwin." He happily recounted to Leni.

"Darwin will do just fine," she said laughing.

"He called me 'brother' and wished us good luck. He has never called me that before."

"He likes you – and so do I."

She kissed him passionately with a sense of relief in her actions.

The other passengers had begun to move to the gate around the passionate couple. One guy who Laurie and Leni had got to know quite well with the IT security project said with a laugh in his voice, "Are you guys going to get on the plane or are you going to stay here have a root."

His mates laughed good naturedly.

The guard opened the gate and the passengers entered the Boeing 737 through the front door after climbing up the primitive set of manually positioned boarding stairs.

When all had boarded, and become seated and the plane had begun its backtrack up the runway, the male purser took up the microphone and said, "Welcome to Australia – Australia starts here!"

This time, there was a cheer and Leni wept tears of joy.

It was a very quiet flight to Darwin. The cabin lights had been switched off and Laurie could see the dark outlines of INTERFET ships, sailing without showing any lights but outlined on the shiny ocean surface. They were heading north.

Nearby passengers could be heard talking about the invasion force below. "There our boys down there," called out one contractor. "And girls," called out a female voice. "Makes you feel just so fuckin proud of our country," said another.

He tried to sleep but he was restless and uneasy. He had already been shot down once by the Indonesian Airforce and was worried that it might happen again.

Their arrival in Darwin was as tedious as one would expect when one arrives without a passport or a visa and with just a letter from the High Commission in Jakarta.

The immigration staff were very supportive. Everybody's mind was on the taskforce heading to East Timor. Leni still referred to it as 'Timor Timur' as it is pronounced in bahasa Indonesian.

Still, nobody knew how the matter of her arrival should be managed. She produced her marriage certificate of only three weeks ago, and questions were asked about whether it was a valid marriage or just a sham for the purpose of getting into Australia.

At one point, a female officer was embarrassed to ask, "The marriage has been consummated, I presume?"

"He consummated me very nicely." Leni replied and all laughed.

Calls were made to Canberra and to the Australian Embassy in Jakarta. In both cases the staff needed were off duty and sleeping at home and so no further processing of her status could be carried out.

Eventually at around 10:30pm, a very senior female immigration officer entered the interview room.

"Mrs Hudson," she began. Leni took a moment to realize that she was talking to her. Nobody had called her that before. She smiled happily.

"There is much in your application that needs to be addressed. We need to understand more about why you feel that you that you need to be granted asylum in Australia and the veracity of your marriage needs to be confirmed. Having said that, I find no reason to deny you entry to Australia but you must understand that you have not yet been granted residency status. It is my decision whether to send you to a detention center or to release you into the community in the recognizance of former Queensland police Senior Sergeant Hudson. I have decided to allow you to stay on the recognizance of Mr Hudson but you must report to the Immigration Office at Pella House 40 Cavenagh Street Darwin, tomorrow at 10:00am."

"Thank you so much!" Leni exclaimed joyously.

"You don't need to thank me – I'm just doing my job," the officer explained. "Welcome to Australia Mrs. Hudson."

The processing of her application took more than a week and they stayed at the travel lodge in the city Centre of Darwin, not far from the Immigration Office. They had plenty of time in between interviews to tour the city. They explored the memorials and sites of the Japanese bombing in world war II as well as the destruction of the city by Cyclone Tracey in 1974. Most of all, Leni enjoyed simply walking the streets of the city and reveling in the freedom and individuality that Darwin more than any other city of the world demonstrates.

An officer of ASIO was called in when it was revealed that Leni had sensitive data that she was prepared to divulge. In that meeting, she revealed the logon ID and password of her XDRIVE account where she revealed the document that had caused her such difficulty.

Soon after that she was given her Temporary Protection Visa.

Since neither of them had very much luggage. Everything that they had previously been travelling with had been lost in the plane crash. So, rather than fly, they decided to buy a motor bike to drive from Darwin to Brisbane. After looking around the city they found a dealer who had an excellent second hand Harley Davidson Road Glide for sale. Laurie decided to buy it.

Leni was overjoyed as she went shopping with Laurie to buy her leathers and helmet to wear on the trip. She bought a black and red jacket with leather tassels along the sleeves and across the back. She also bought matching gloves, a cruiser helmet and matching boots. Laurie also bought his gear, no tassels and all black.

They had a great time travelling to Brisbane making many stops along the way especially in Mt Isa and Longreach where they spent two nights in each location. They went swimming and kayaking in Lake Moondarra in Mt Isa and wandered about in amazement as they enjoyed the sights and sounds of the Stockman's Hall of Fame in Longreach.

They decided to live in a house that Laurie owned at Caloundra. It is a delightful beach side city about an hour's drive north of Brisbane. Laurie's house was very comfortable having three bedrooms and a view over the water. Although to the north of the city of Brisbane, the coast line was curved and had a promontory on which the house was constructed and so the view from the main window actually looked south. Because the maritime traffic needed to avoid nearby islands and to find a deep-water passage, the shipping lane passed near the shore and it was a very enjoyable pastime lying on the verandah and watching the passage of the ships.

In addition to their Harley, they also purchased a Toyota Aurion Presara after they arrived in Brisbane. This was a luxuriously appointed vehicle with soft leather seats, woodgrain paneling, a sunroof and a very powerful six-cylinder motor. They needed to make the hour-long trip to Brisbane city quite frequently for various reasons but mostly for interviews with the Department of Immigration. She did not have an Indonesian passport other than the "stolen" one that her cousin had provided. She did have her "Kartu Tanda

Penduduk" which was commonly referred to as a KTP, it is an Indonesian identity card which all adult citizens must carry.

Laurie and Leni made it very clear to the officers of the Department of Immigration that her whereabouts must not be given to the Indonesian officials in view of the danger that she was in. There were ASIO Officers, particularly the ones who interviewed her in Darwin, who also reiterated this fact to the department.

She went through the process of being granted her spouse based citizenship which eventually included her being required to complete the Australian Citizenship Examination. Some three months later, she was advised that she could collect her Citizen Certificate from the Department of Immigration in Adelaide Street in the city.

They could have asked for it to be posted to them but Leni needed to have one of her teeth root filled because an abscess had formed beneath it. This was likely to have been the result of her having been hit on the jaw by the raskol. She had made an appointment to visit a periodontist on Wickham Terrace to get the procedure carried out. The dentist's rooms were nearby to the Immigration Department so they made an appointment to pick up her certificate from the office.

They drove down from Caloundra and parked in the Wickham Terrace car park. Leni went to the periodontist while Laurie had a coffee. Then they collected her certificate from the department and began the drive back to Caloundra. They expected the trip to take around ninety minutes since they needed to drive through the city traffic before reaching the north of the city and joining the M1 to drive to Caloundra.

Chapter 15 – Attacked When Least Expected.

They were Travelling on a 110mph section of the motorway just north of the town of Burpengary. Laurie was driving and Leni was bemoaning the fact that her root canal work was going to cost about $2,000.

"Look!" Laurie exclaimed, "I have very few other expenses and I can afford it. If I can spend a few bucks so that the woman that I love can chew comfortably, it will be worth it."

He was glancing in his rear-view mirrors from time to time, as he spoke, to remain aware of the traffic around him being the sensible driver that he was. Leni had lain her seat back and was relaxing comfortably. He was travelling in the center lane and was slowly gaining on a car that was travelling in the left lane some one hundred metres ahead. The right lane was clear but for a motorcycle that was about fifty metres behind him. There was a solid metal guard rail that ran along the right of the road which was to prevent vehicles running into the ditch that separated the northbound and southbound lanes.

He saw the motorcycle disappear from view in his central rear view mirror as it began to pull beside him and he was vaguely conscious of it's becoming visible in his right external mirror.

Suddenly, his side window shattered and he heard a bang from the sunroof where something had hit it. Leni screamed and Laurie turned to look through the hole in his shattered window only to see the cyclist pointing a gun at him. As a man who had fired many a pistol in his life and as one who had also ridden a motorbike his brain suddenly went into an instinctive mode and he rapidly swung the car to the right in order to collide with the gunman. He knew that with a car swinging towards him, the rider would move his gun hand back down to the handlebar so as to better control the bike.

He could see the rider holding both the hand grip of the handle bar and the pistol in his left hand. Laurie was determined to keep that hand there and not to let the would-be assassin get in another shot. He continued to swing the Toyota to the right and he heard the impact as the side of his car impacted with the cycle. It came as no surprise for him to see the rider slowing down but Laurie was determined to keep pushing the cycle to the guard rail and so he carefully braked so as to stay abreast of the rider. He was soon to hear a gut-wrenching howl as the rider found himself being pushed against the rail. All control was lost of the cycle with the rider being flung off and the bike cartwheeling through the air before it flipped over the guardrail and skidded to a stop in the ditch.

Laurie carefully pulled back over the left two lanes and pulled to a stop on the left of the motorway. He consoled Leni who was very shocked and was bleeding from her left arm. He waited for the police to arrive.

They didn't.

He dialed 000 on his phone and reported that there was a traffic accident involving a death and gave his location.

After many minutes a police car arrived.

The two offices, a man and a woman, pulled up behind the Toyota.

The male constable had a face red with fury at what he saw was the negligent killing of a motorcyclist.

He walked to the driver's door and in a voice, that could melt steel, said coldly, "Get out of the car please sir."

This was not a simple procedure since the door of the Toyota was badly damaged and eventually required both Laurie pushing from the inside and the cop pulling

143

from the outside. After opening the door, the highway patrol officer said, "Stand with your hands on the roof of your vehicle. I am arresting you for dangerous driving causing death."

"You have every right to do that constable but I assert that the motorcyclist was shooting at me. I request that your colleague examines the wreck of the motorcycle and somewhere before that point, she will find a recently fired pistol. Moreover, I request that you impound this vehicle and take it for forensic examination. Somewhere, possibly in the hood lining near the sunroof, you will find a bullet."

The female officer was assisting Leni who was still sobbing loudly out of the car. "You don't need to look for the bullet, here it is." She said.

They all looked at the Leni who was bleeding from her left arm. She pulled out the battered projectile from where it had partly lodged in the flesh of her upper arm and close to her body. She handed it to the female officer whereupon she turned away and vomited.

"I think that this rather changes the situation," said the much-mollified constable.

"I think so too," said Laurie, as he began walking back up the highway and, after waiting for some traffic to clear, crossed over to the wreckage of the motorcycle.

The rider had been decapitated by the guardrail and blood ran down over the grey zinc plated steel and formed an irregular pool on the ground.

"If you look back there, you should find the gun," Laurie said pointing back up the lane.

The officer made his way back for a short distance before deciding that it was too dangerous walking on the right-hand lane of the motorway. He called up on his radio for assistance. A second vehicle arrived a couple of minutes later and with blue and red lights flashing blocked the lane.

While this was happening, Laurie crouched beside the headless body and felt in the inside jacket of the rider. As he had hoped, he found an Indonesian passport in the pocket. He removed it quickly and read the name.

"Yudianto Hidayat" it read. His address was shown as being in Kebayoran Baru which Laurie knew was a suburb of Jakarta.

A female sergeant was in the second vehicle accompanied by another male constable. Whether by accident or design, the second vehicle had parked, with high intensity lights flashing, in the right-hand lane and so close to the guard rail that the wide hipped and heavy set sergeant had difficulty squeezing out of the driver's door. The effect however was not to block the lane and the constable immediately set about to direct the traffic past the incident site and to attempt to discourage ghoulish drivers from slowing down for a look at the carnage.

The constable began walking slowly towards the newly arrived vehicle and was scouring the ground for the gun. He had taken about fifty steps before he came to a section of the guardrail that had been heavily scratched and with the paint from the motorcycle rubbed off onto it. This was clearly the point of impact where the cyclist first contacted the rail. Laurie watched him stoop over the rail and after about a minute of scratching about, the cop stood and held up the pistol hanging by the trigger guard from a short stick which the officer had thoughtfully found nearby and which he had used to avoid contaminating any prints on the weapon.

This was clearly not the usual situation that the highway patrol officers were accustomed to. The sergeant and Laurie joined the cop with the gun at the same moment and she was obviously rattled by this discovery.

Very unprofessionally, she exclaimed, "What the fuck is going on here?"

Laurie looked at the name badge pinned above the bulge of the sergeants very large right breast and addressed her by that name.

"Sergeant McBride," he began, "There are a few things that I should make you aware of."

The woman stared at him and said nothing but her expression made it clear that she wanted him to continue.

"My name is Laurie Hudson and you can find some of my records in the Police staff database because I used to work for the QPS. I was also a senior sergeant when I left."

He looked at the woman and she looked back at him and nodded. He handed her the passport which he had taken from the body. McBride frowned at him for interfering with the corpse but said nothing.

Laurie continued, "I am in Australia with my wife, Leni, who is a refugee from Indonesia. She has only today been granted Australian citizenship. You can see from the gun that the constable is holding and from the bullet wound and indeed the bullet itself that your companion is holding that we have been attacked. We have reason to believe that this assassin is working for rogue elements of Kopassis, the Indonesian Special Forces Command, who want my wife dead. The Australian Federal Police have investigated this matter and, as I said, Mrs Hudson has just today been granted Australian Citizenship. I suggest that you may want to refer this matter to them."

"Thanks Laurie," she replied, "Are you the guy that they used to call Truck?"

"They still do." He laughed.

"I had only just graduated when you left the service, I was sorry to hear about your wife and son."

"Thank you!"

She turned to the constable still holding the gun by the stick.

"Andrew, you did well to not contaminate that thing with your prints but you will need to take care of it until forensics arrive because I want to be sure that there is no doubt in linking it to that dead bastard over there"

The female constable had been making her way across the highway and had just caught up with the group after leaving Leni alone in the Toyota.

"Hi Yvonne," said the sergeant, "How is Mrs. Hudson?"

The young woman opened her eyes widely with a expression that indicated that she was learning Leni's surname for the first time and replied, "She is very shocked but the bleeding of her arm has stopped."

"Has the bullet lodged in her arm?" Her sergeant asked.

"No Boss, I have it here." She unfolded a bloody tissue that she was clinging to in her hand and revealed the very misshapen projectile.

As she presented it, she remarked, "It must have got bent up as it passed through the window and bounced off the roof of the car."

"Can you see where it bounced off the roof?"

"Oh Yes! The hood lining is torn and there is a deep scratch there."

Suddenly McBride stood at her full height. It was clear that she had decided what to do and she took charge.

"Yvonne, go back to your vehicle and call an ambulance to take care of Mrs. Hudson. Tell them that we also have a deceased here but the body cannot be moved yet pending forensics examination."

Then she turned to Yvonne's partner who was still holding the gun.

"Andrew, get in my vehicle and call in accident forensics and tell them to get a crew here fast."

Then she turned to the young constable who had been travelling with her.

"Phil, get the tarps out of our car and cover the body and the head of this shooter. Then start putting the witches hats out to close off this lane."

She directed her attention back at Laurie. "How come the rider ran into the guard rail?" she asked.

"He was shooting at me."

"Why didn't you try to speed up or swerve away?"

"Motorcycles have better acceleration and are more maneuverable than a car. I would not have been able to get away."

"So, you deliberately swerved into him to knock him off his bike."

"He missed on his first shot, I didn't want to let him fire again."

"They said that you were a tough bastard, Truck, they were right."

Then she took a mobile phone from her pocket and pressed a speed dial number and soon Laurie heard her say to the person at the other end.

"Sir, do remember a senior sergeant named Laurie Hudson?"

...

"Yes, Truck, that's him," She looked at Laurie and grinned.

"Sir, I've got him with me on the northbound M1, just north of Burpengary. He was attacked by an Indonesian national riding a motorcycle who attempted to shoot him. He swerved into the cyclist in defense of himself and his wife who is also an Indonesian national now with Australian citizenship."

...

"Yes! He is fine but Mrs Hudson was hit by the bullet and she suffered a minor wound."

...

Yes Sir, this is not a traffic accident but an attempted assassination of an Australian Citizen by a foreign national. I think that you might want to get your people here quickly and also call in the AFP. Truck says that the Australian Federal Police are already involved with this case and this is why his wife, has been granted residency.

...

"That's right, so I have blocked off the lane of the highway and secured the crime scene and we have recovered the gun and the bullet."

...

"No sir, we have not contaminated the gun, my officer picked it up with a stick through the trigger guard."

...

"That's good, Sir, we need to get this cleaned up as soon as possible, we can't keep a lane of the M1 closed indefinitely. I look forward to seeing your crew within half an hour."

The sound of an ambulance siren could be heard in the distance and McBride said," OK Truck, you'd better go with your wife in the ambulance when it gets here. The homicide guys and the AFP will want to catch up with you for a statement. Just so you know, I will be reporting that I found you in your car with your wife who has a minor bullet wound. We found the deceased with a wrecked bike and a gun on the side of the road. All the evidence suggests that you were an innocent victim of a failed assassination attempt.

The ambulance arrived and Leni was placed on a stretcher and given oxygen since, although her injury was minor, she was very shocked by the attack. Laurie rode in the front of the ambulance after declining any treatment.

He had recovered his laptop from the Toyota and typed out a statement of what had happened as he sat in the waiting room while waiting for Leni's wound to be treated.

He had finished typing and was proof reading the document when two officers entered the waiting room. One beamed at him and shook him fondly by the hand.

"Truck, mate! It is great to see you again," said Inspector David Holland of the Queensland police.

"Great to see you again too." Laurie replied.

Holland turned to the AFP officer. "Truck, this is Senior Sergeant Max Gould of the AFP.

Since Gould was in uniform and had three chevrons and a crown encased in wattle sprigs on his epaulet the introduction by rank was unnecessary but was a courtesy.

Gould held out his hand and Laurie shook it. "David has been telling me about when you and he worked together. I am sorry to hear that you are no longer in uniform."

It was an oblique way of saying that he knew why he left the service and Laurie graciously responded, "Life must go on."

Laurie realized that two such senior officers would not be involved in a roadside shooting even one that resulted in death. But when the matter was split between Federal and State jurisdictions and with potential international repercussions there would be a need for it to be given a high profile. He also knew that, friendly as Holland was, he would be meticulous in the investigation. They were a good pair when they worked together so long ago. Laurie was the one who would come up with intuitive, even brilliant, 'out of the box' ideas to figure out a crime while Holland displayed great attention to detail and this combined with his amazing memory enabled him to figure out what had happened at least as often as Laurie would do.

They began to discuss the incident just a Leni emerged with her arm in a sling. Laurie introduced her to the two officers.

After the introductions, Laurie said, "Guys, I would like to get Leni home. How about if you drive us to my house and I will print out a statement on my printer that I have already typed up on my laptop here."

It was a short trip from the Caloundra Hospital to Laurie's house on the hill near the famous lighthouse. They sat together in the rear of the black Commonwealth Ford Fairlane. As promised, Laurie printed off the statement. Not surprisingly it was in just the format that the officers required.

Holland asked, "When the bullet came through the window, why did you swing the car to the right and impact the motorcycle?"

"I heard Leni scream and I thought that she was warning me that there was someone on my left. It was an instinctive reaction."

Holland smiled. "Of course," he replied. He knew and Gould knew that he had deliberately killed the attempted assassin. They could charge Laurie but even if it could be proved that it was deliberate, no jury would convict someone who acted to save his life and that of his partner who had been wounded by an attacker with a gun.

After they had confirmed a few details with Laurie and Leni and they both signed the statement, the two officers departed.

Laurie noticed that he had received an email while he had been printing the statement. He went back to his laptop to read it after the police had departed.

It was from an unknown and very likely untraceable email address. It said;

My vriend,

Take care! They know that you are in Oz.

Watch out for a guy named Yudianto Hidayat.

Here is his picture.

Cheers

Jakob_regop10inch

Attached to Johan's email was the picture from Hidayat's passport.

Laurie replied back;

Baie dankie Mate,

We already met this bastard – he is dead.

Will let you know what we decide to do.

Thanks again

Laurie and Leni.

"What are we going to do?" asked Leni.

"Fucked if I know." replied Laurie.

They watched the news that night and an item came on saying how a motorcyclist had been side swiped on the M1 by a car and was killed on impact with the guard rail. "Police are calling on motorists to be more aware of motorcyclists and not to change lanes without looking. Speed was also a factor in this accident and remember that every 'K' over is a killer"

Chapter 16 – Trouble at Sea

They stayed in Laurie's house at Caloundra for the next three months and felt like prisoners.

Laurie noticed that police vehicles cruised down their street fairly frequently and they always went very slowly past their house. Other vehicles which he hoped were unmarked police cars did the same.

They enrolled in a gun club and eventually got a license to hold some rifles and a pistol.

Luckily, there was a couple who lived in the house next door and the wife was also of Chinese descent. Her name was Wendy Collins (nee Chan) and her husband's name was Brian. Wendy could speak Mandarin but hadn't done so since she got married five years ago. She enjoyed speaking to her new friend in the language of her childhood. She still held the family love of Mahjong and the two couples would play each week. Laurie picked up the rules but never displayed the skill that the two women possessed. Both men were amused at the passion that their partners displayed for this game and would smile good naturedly whenever they got berated for not noticing a subtle move that their opponents had made.

What did annoy Laurie was when Leni confided her story to Wendy. He felt that this would expose them to further risk but he eventually understood his woman's need to confide in and enjoy the friendship of another woman. Brian was a nice guy, a retired Air Force pilot, and he and Laurie would go fishing in his small boat and they loved putting crab pots in the nearby Bells Creek.

One day, as Laurie and Leni were driving north along the Nicklin highway to have lunch at the Kawana Waters Hotel, Leni noticed an adult store along the way.

"What is an 'adult store'?" she asked Laurie. "I saw one in Bulcock Street as well, do they sell adults?" she laughed at the absurdity of what she suggested.

"Do you really not know?"

"I wouldn't be asking you if I did, I have never seen one before."

Laurie laughed, "They sell sex toys and products. They call them 'adult stores' because children can't go in."

"OH! That sounds like fun, can we go there on the way home?"

"I've got a better idea, why don't you take Wendy. You two girls will really enjoy shopping there."

So, the following day, the enthusiastic Leni and the somewhat more guarded, Wendy went shopping."

They spent almost an hour shopping in the store looking at the range of erotic DVDs and various toys, that would fit in either orifice and in some cases, both. There was a great assortment of dress up costumes along with a plethora of lubricants and lotions.

Leni took great delight in showing Laurie her purchases when she got home. She had bought some his and hers lubricant which when the two were mixed together would become quite warm and scintillating for both parties. She was eager to schedule a 'special occasion' when they could try it out. She also bought some nipple ornaments including a pair of bells. What surprised Laurie the most was the set of handcuffs and ankle chains joined by a chain which would totally immobilize her if she was made to wear it.

"Are you sure that you would enjoy being chained up with this?" he asked.

"Absolutely! It would be great fun," she replied giggling.

As they lay together absolutely satiated from the intense love making that they had very recently enjoyed, Laurie remarked to the woman who lay beside him still with her wrists and ankles cuffed, "I think that you are amazing. I have never known a woman with as intense a love of sex as you have."

Leni laughed and replied, "I'm just doing what my mother used to say."

"What's that?"

"If you drain his balls every day,
Your man will never ever stray."

Very amused by this, Laurie asked, "Surely you don't think that I would stray after all that we have been through together."

"Of course not, I just so love making love to you."

"But what surprises me is that you are always wanting to do it in different ways, and now that you have discovered this adult shop, you have become a real sex fiend."

"Mother says that sex is like food. If you keep giving your man rice he will get bored. It is the same with sex. God gives women three holes and two hands that she can entertain her man with. If she loves him, she will use all of them."

"I'd like to meet your mother one day. She must be an interesting lady"

"Yes – that would be a good idea, we should do it as soon as it is safe.

"OK!"

Not surprisingly, Laurie and Leni enjoyed some very interesting evenings after that. Laurie thought about asking what Wendy had purchased, but Leni didn't mention it and so he didn't ask.

Leni made subsequent visits to many of the similar stores that dotted the Sunshine Coast and always came home with something interesting to experiment with.

The two women would occasionally ride with the boys in Brian's boat and would enjoy swimming and sunbaking whenever the water was calm and the weather was nice. Both girls would become seasick whenever there was the slightest turbulence in the water. Moreover, they could never understand the massive

155

effort that the men put into trying to catch crabs when in the main all that they caught were jennies (females) who could not be kept by law and likewise, undersize bucks. On the rare occasions that they caught a legally edible crab one would have thought that the boys had won the lottery.

Caloundra's main street, Bulcock Street, would become a street mall every Sunday. They would always visit it and the girls would buy bits and pieces from the many craft stores. Also, they would enjoy the food from the many food outlets which covered a plethora of ethnic tastes.

Laurie felt that the large crowd in the street would deter any potential attacker however, he was on full alert as they walked. He tried to hide his concern from Leni and Wendy who enjoyed the shopping and it was important that he should try to make life for her as normal as he could.

There was an incident where a young guy came at them with a large knife. Laurie sprang into action and in a smooth display of Asian style self-defense, he kicked the knife from the assumed attacker's hand and quickly seized the guy by forcing his arm up behind his back while holding onto his throat with his other hand. It turned out that the young fool was working at a nearby food store selling meat. He was going to offer the group the knife so that they could cut a sample off the roast that he was selling.

It soon became obvious that there had been a misunderstanding and Laurie released the guy.

"Don't go waving knives around in public," Laurie cautioned, "People can get the wrong idea."

"Who are you?" the young vendor asked angrily, "Some sort of secret fucking agent."

"Some sort." Laurie replied as they quickly walked away surrounded by a buzz of conversation from curious onlookers.

The same guy was there again the following week but Laurie noticed that the knife was now left on the table and he was touting for business with his hands empty. Laurie nodded to him and the guy smiled. Wendy bought some of his meat as a gesture of goodwill and which turned out to be a good thing to do because it was remarkably tasty.

He always made sure that the house was securely locked whenever he left Leni at home and most times she had Wendy with her.

They had been living at Caloundra for close to four months when the two couples again went out in the boat together.

Golden beach fronts on to a large water course called "Pumice Stone Passage". It is the sound that separates the large island called "Bribie" from the Australian mainland. At Golden Beach, the passage is a couple of miles wide and, whilst never impassible, it has a variety of magnificent white sandbanks which are continually forming and reforming in various combinations, often as Islands in the channel or as peninsulas extending sometimes from the mainland or sometimes from the island.

Some parts of the sandbanks are accessible at all times but most parts are only available at low tide.

Laurie and Brian had anchored the boat at a sandbank which had formed as a long peninsula extending from the beach of Bribie. The girls had been swimming in the warm tranquil water and sunbaking on the soft white sand. They had shed their tiny bikini tops and were enjoying the feeling of the soft warm sun on their breasts.

The men had been fishing without very much success until the tide turned and suddenly the fish began biting and they began to catch a few nice sized whiting.

The sandbank began to shrink in size and the girls had got dressed, if you could call wearing tiny bikinis dressed, and they began to load the boat. With the fish still biting, the men continued to fish as the sandbank became completely covered by water. It was not until they were standing in knee deep water that they gave up and stashed their fishing rods in the boat and climbed in themselves.

Brian retrieved and stowed the anchor while Laurie started the outboard motor. As the little boat moved off, Brian noticed that a much larger cabin cruiser that had been moored near the middle of the passage began to move also. As Laurie steered the boat away from the Island, the larger boat adjusted its course towards them.

Laurie, sitting in the stern of the boat had his forward vision obscured by the two women sitting on the middle seat as well as by Brian sitting on the bow. He did not notice the cabin cruiser heading towards them, now at considerable speed, until Brian pointed it out.

"Shit!" Laurie exclaimed as he pulled the outboard about to turn the boat hard into a starboard "U" turn. He pushed the throttle to full speed which despite the howling of the motor was less than five knots.

He headed to the submerged sandbank hoping to cross it and put a barrier between themselves and the much larger and deeper draft cabin cruiser.

He crossed the bar with the propeller whipping up sand as it bounced along the bottom. He was intending to head for the beach of the island where he hoped that they could get ashore before the large fast moving boat would bash their small boat to pieces. He hoped that they might be able escape their pursuers by hiding in the scrub that separated the still water beach on their side of the island from the surf beach on the other side.

He expected that the cabin cruiser would swing away from the sandbank and go around it and then use its speed in an effort to intercept their boat before they made landfall.

He looked back at their pursuers and saw the cruiser with its bow high as it sped rapidly towards them. With its bow so high, its driver would not have been able to see their small boat now so close and so low in the water. There was a guy squatting on the bow waving instructions to the driver to assist him setting a course to slice through their much smaller craft.

Suddenly the guy in the bow saw the sandbank and stood and waved desperately to the driver to turn away. He was too late.

Laurie and the others watched in amazement as the cabin cruiser hit the sand bar with a terrifying crash. It went from some thirty knots to zero in about five feet.

The guy at the bow flew through the air with arms and legs flailing before he landed in the water some fifty feet ahead of his boat. If he had simply tried to stand, he could have touched the bottom in the water which was chest to neck deep. Instead, he was obviously unable to swim and he continued to flail around in panic. He was howling in Bahasa Indonesian for help. Soon as he gulped and inhaled more and more the screaming stopped and he became still and disappeared below the surface

The four friends could not see what had happened to the driver. Very likely, he would have been thrown against the console or the windscreen at great speed and would be either unconscious or dead. The motor was screaming at top revs and it appeared that the gearbox or the propeller had sheared. Running at full power and with no load, it would only be a short matter of time before it destroyed itself.

Laurie's outboard was still running at its less than impressive full speed but was safely carrying them away from the impact site.

"Shouldn't we try to rescue them?" Wendy asked.

"Who?" asked Laurie grim faced as he turned the small craft towards the boat ramp at Golden beach where their car and boat trailer had been parked.

They watched the local news that night and it was reported that a cabin cruiser hired by a visitor to Australia from Indonesia had been found sinking after hitting a sandbank at high speed. It was reported that two men had hired the boat but only the body of one man was found with severe head injuries in the boat. Police are looking for the second man.

Back at the house, Laurie took out his iPhone and rang a number. When it answered, he was heard to say, Can I speak to Inspector David Holland please?

...

"Just tell him it is Truck."

...

"Mate! You'd better meet me, there is something that I must tell you."

Chapter 17 – What to Do Now

David Holland visited the house in his private car and sat and enjoyed a cup of tea and the slices of boiled fruit cake that Wendy had made.

Laurie had briefed the Inspector about the assassination attempt in his phone call, the day before and Holland was now updating the group on what had occurred since.

Laurie was not happy about further involving Brian and Wendy but they had insisted.

"We were in that boat too!" Brian protested. "This involves us now."

After the pleasantries, had been concluded and David was sitting addressing the group while balancing a cup and saucer of tea on his knee and holding a slice of fruit cake in his other hand, he began to address the four survivors.

"You will be happy to know, that the Water Police have confirmed your account of what happened, not that there was any doubt," he said looking at Laurie.

"The Cabin Cruiser had been stolen from the Pacific Harbor Marina on Bribie Island. It hit the sandbank with such force that structural damage was done to the hull and the boat is to be scrapped." There was a body in the cabin. He was known to us with links to a motorcycle gang with a reputation for drug trafficking, violent stand over tactics and suspected murder. He clearly killed himself when he was thrown against the console. The other guy was only found this morning. His body was carried south by the incoming tide and was found floating about a mile north of the Bribie bridge. There was water in his lungs – he died of drowning. He has been identified as an Indonesian national who was in Australia on a tourist visa. He arrived on the exact same flight as your earlier acquaintance, Mr. Hidayat."

"What was this guy's name?" Laurie asked."

"Randika Hasan was the name that he travelled under." Replied the police officer.

"Wendy was sobbing. "Why can't you just keep them away from us?" she cried.

"The first thing that we must do is for us to get away from you," Laurie said to the distraught woman. "It is Leni that they want to kill and having you guys near us creates a risk for you."

"I'm a risk to all of you." Leni exclaimed with tears rolling down her cheeks. "I just need to go away by myself. I can't have the people that I love put in danger." She stared at Laurie and said, "That includes you!"

"Don't be silly!" exclaimed Laurie. "I promised to look after you and I will."

"Even if it kills you?" she asked looking into his eyes.

Laurie changed the subject and turned his attention to David, "How did these bastards know that we were here?"

"That's the problem, "David replied, shaking his head, "We just don't know. Obviously, these rogue Kopassus bastards have got links into the Australian system. As you know, there has been defense and police co-operation between the two countries for decades, and even now with relations at their lowest ebb there are still groups and individuals that are still talking. It seems to me that these rogues are getting information from the immigration Department, the AFP or the Queensland police."

"Or all three?" ventured Laurie.

"Or all three." Conceded David.

There was silence as the group sat deep in thought. Wendy and Leni were hugging each other and sobbing.

Eventually, Laurie looked at David and asked, "Mate do you think that you could fast track an Aussie passport for Leni?"

The officer looked at his friend with a look that indicated that he knew what he was thinking. "Well, as you know, that is outside my jurisdiction, but I will have a chat to Max Gould. Under the circumstances, I shouldn't think that that will be much of a problem."

"Where will we go?" asked Leni.

"I don't know yet but having an Australian passport is a start." Her friend and lover replied. He looked at David as he spoke.

David nodded his head in understanding. He realized that Laurie had made up his mind about where he would go and he was sure that he knew what he had in mind. He was aware that there was no reason for Laurie to tell him what he had planned and under the circumstances, the fewer people who knew about it, the better.

"Well, I'd best be going," David said. "I will give Gould a call when I get back to my office. Also, don't be alarmed if you see even more marked police cars patrolling this street until you leave. I do want to catch up with you before you go."

He stood and shook hands with the two women, again thanking Wendy for the fruit cake as he did so. Likewise, he shook hands with Brian before giving a man hug to Laurie.

Holding his friend with a hand firmly grasping each shoulder, David spoke softly and with emphasis, "Let's get this shit behind us as soon as we can. I'm retiring in a couple of years and I want to join you guys fishing from that boat of yours."

"You will be very welcome, Mate!" Laurie replied.

The policeman left and Leni then asked Laurie what he had planned.

"I'm making this up as I go along," he replied dismissively. "The first thing that we must do is to get your passport application lodged."

Soon after, Leni and Laurie borrowed Brian's car and drove to the nearby Caloundra Village shopping Centre where Leni had her photograph taken at the post office. Laurie signed and certified the photo's as a former police officer. They completed the remainder of the passport application form. They handed it to the postal clerk and paid for it with Laurie's Visa card.

They had been back at the house for about two hours. Leni was making some noodles and Laurie was trawling the web looking at travel sites. His phone rang;

"Laurie speaking." He answered.

"Max Gould."

"Hi Max, how are you?"

"Good, I hear you need a passport expedited."

"Yes, I do. I guess that you know what happened yesterday."

"A shit of a business. Mate! I've just got to say how gutted I feel to know that we can't protect you in your own country."

"Yes! We are just a bit pissed off ourselves."

"As you should be. Listen, there is something that you need to know."

"What's that?"

"We've been following up on your pals, Hidayat and Hasan. You've picked some pretty highly placed bastards to play with. They both report to sorry, reported to, a guy named Ibraham Setepu. This bastard is the deputy head of Kopassus and his pal is a retired General named Makarim. This corrupt bastard is an aspirant for the National Presidency. I have met Setepu a couple of times and he heads up a group which we know sympathizes with Islamic terrorists. We can't prove it and nobody in Indonesia can either. He has the support of President Habibie not only because he is

Moslem but because Habibie is weak and is unable to garner sufficient support to have his own guys in control.

"OK – thanks for the heads up. I am hoping that I can get Leni away to where he can't find her."

"Speaking of that, has she lodged her passport application?"

"Yes! Did it today at the Caloundra Village Post Office."

"Good – I will take care of it."

"Thanks Max. I guess that I will see you later."

"You will! Take care, goodbye."

"Goodbye."

Laurie pressed off the phone.

He turned to Leni. "Do you know of a guy named Ibraham Setepu?"

"Oh Yes! – He works at the Defense Headquarters and is the guy that was to have got the message that I accidentally intercepted."

"Ah Ha! – Well Max has discovered that he is the guy to whom our two would be killers report to."

"That makes sense," she replied, "but since you didn't let me see Hidayat's head and all that I saw of Hasan was when he went flying through the air before he hit the water. So, I really don't know if I had ever seen them anywhere around the defense offices."

She paused before asking, "So what do we do now?"

"What we do now my sweet is that we go and have a nice shower before we go to bed to celebrate still being alive."

She smiled, "I think that this is a special occasion."

"Do you want it to be?"

"I think that being so smart to drive over the sandbank deserves a special reward."

She squealed in delight as he picked her up and carried her to the bathroom.

Chapter 18 – Friends in High Places

They received notification to collect their passport from the Post Office three weeks later.

David had been good to his promise and there had been a strong police presence in the area during that time. Sometimes a marked police car would park in front of their house and the officers inside would sit and drink a coffee.

The Aurion Presara had finally been returned from the police and Laurie had taken it to the local panel beaters to have the door and side panels repaired. Brian had undertaken to look after selling the car on ebay and would deposit the money in Laurie's account when it was sold. Laurie gave them the Harley and the helmets and leathers to enjoy until they returned.

Secretly, Laurie gave a set of signed undated papers for the sale of the Harley to Brian. "If you don't hear from us for two years of if you hear that we are dead, I want you to date these documents and enjoy the bike with my best wishes."

Laurie bounced away any questions from Leni about where they were going by saying; "I don't know yet."

As soon as the passport arrived, Laurie became very busy planning things on his laptop. He had a long discussion with Brian as well as yet another call to Max Gould.

"OK! My love, here is the plan, let me know what you think of it." He said to his wife as they finished off a delightful homemade pizza that they had become very adept to making to their own recipe.

"I guessed that you must be getting close to getting it figured out because you haven't been on the computer all day today. Where are we going?"

"South Africa."

"Oh." Followed by a long pause. "When do we go?"

So, Laurie explained the plan. He had booked flights from Brisbane to Perth. His flight left in one week's time at 8am and her flight left the following day at Midday. He wanted them to fly separately to reduce the risk of them being identified as a couple. The flights had been booked under the names of Brian and Wendy. Brian had lent Laurie their Visa card and passports which Laurie had used to book the flights. Laurie had refunded the cost of the fares back to Brian in cash.

It was a domestic flight to Perth so there was no requirement for a passport.

They were also booked to fly separately to South Africa on Qantas. Again, Laurie was to leave one day and Leni was to leave one day later. Max had instructed them to arrive at the Qantas check in at Perth Airport at exactly 10:15 am both days.

Laurie had said that they couldn't fly out on a false passport because the Qantas booking clerk will check that the photograph on the passport matches that of the passenger. "Don't worry," Max had replied. "Just make sure that you get there at exactly 10:15."

Similarly, they were instructed to be sure to go through Immigration Exit Gate '3' when they checked through into the sterile area where the gate lounges were.

When they arrived in South Africa, they would be beyond any assistance that Max could provide and that they would be on their own. Laurie was to enter the RSA on his South African passport and Leni should then use her new Australian passport.

"How come we won't get stopped in Perth when we try to use passports that are not ours." Leni asked.

"Airlines only check passports to make sure that the traveler won't get rejected at the other end and then require the airline to have to bring them back. Also, leaving Australia on a false passport is not a crime but

167

the AFP will check passports to ensure that criminals are not trying to leave the country to avoid prosecution. I don't really know about this stuff but Max assures me that it is all OK." Laurie explained.

On the Wednesday, one week later, Leni drove Laurie to the Brisbane airport in Brian's car. They embraced fondly before he got out of the car. "See you in prison," she said laughing. More seriously, she said, "call me as soon as you can."

"OK – love you."

"Love you too!"

Laurie checked in to the flight to Perth using Brian's Qantas card at the terminal and checked in his suitcase at the automated baggage drop and after clearing security, he was on his way to the gate lounge without making any human contact at all.

He had done the tedious four and one half hour flight from Brisbane to Perth many times. He had spotted a Lee Child novel that he hadn't read before at the book exchange in Bulcock street Caloundra. He had bought it and stored it in his computer bag to take on the flight. He passed away the hours deep in the exciting world of Jack Reacher righting yet another injustice with a damsel on his arm.

On arrival at Perth, he could have stayed at any of the cheap hotels near the airport but he decided to indulge himself and stay at the Parmelia Hilton in Mill Street in the city. He had often stayed there in the past and always found the meals and the customer service to be excellent.

His limousine got him back to the airport at 9:30am. He hung around until exactly 10:15am before going to the check in desk. He waited behind another passenger before reaching the counter. The very pleasant check in girl smiled warmly but as soon as she read his name, she turned and made eye contact with a guy wearing a black suit and who had an ear plug in his ear. He nodded and she quickly went through the check in process. She asked for his passport but she did not open it. She gave him his boarding pass with the usual smile and wishes for a lovely trip. Laurie saw her look to the guy again after she ran the feeder belt which scooted his suitcase onto the main baggage conveyer but the guy was already moving away.

After passing through security and placing his laptop back in the carry bag, he headed straight for the immigration gates. There were two people at gate three. One person was a regular uniformed official but the other was the same guy in the black suit. He walked up to the booth and presented the immigration form that he had earlier filled out to the uniformed officer. As before, the officer looked at the guy in the suit after he read the name on the form. And, just as before, the guy nodded and the officer took the passport, boarding pass and form and stamped the form which he put in a box along with hundreds of others and opened the passport but he did not look at the page in the passport that had Brian's photograph.

As Laurie moved away from the booth, the guy in the suit caught up with him.

"Mr Hudson," the guy said as he flashed his badge discretely, "Do you have a passport that might not be yours?"

Not knowing what was to happen next, Laurie handed Brian's passport to the guy.

"Senior Sergeant Gould has asked me to collect this so that it can be returned to its owner. Have a nice trip!" The guy said as he turned and walked away

Laurie phoned Leni from the gate lounge knowing that she would be waiting to board her plane in Brisbane. He gave her a heads-up on the process that he had just experienced in order to help her feel more relaxed when she did it.

He hadn't bought a business class ticket for the flight to Perth but he did for the eight-hour flight from Perth to Johannesburg. He relaxed and enjoyed the comfortable Qantas seat/bed and the excellent food and customer service. He watched the movies, 'Star Wars – The Phantom Menace' and "Eyes Wide Shut'. For the remaining time, he dozed away the long flight. He enjoyed a Bundaberg Rum and coke soon after he boarded and he had two glasses of wine with his dinner but other than that, he had no other drinks as he wanted to be fully alert when he arrived in Johannesburg.

He had no difficulty on arrival at Johannesburg and passed swiftly through immigration with his South African passport. He caught a shuttle bus to the Protea Hotel near the airport where he had previously made a booking. He settled in to wait for Leni.

Leni arrived the following day as planned. Since she was travelling on an Australian passport, she needed to pass through immigration. As the wife of an RSA citizen, she was entitled to residency. There was some discussion about this by the staff and Laurie got involved and needed to vouch that she was indeed his wife even though Leni had produced their marriage certificate. Eventually, it was agreed that she would be given an immediate Ninety-day tourist residency during which time, her permanent residency would be processed and granted within thirty days.

"Don't expect anything much by thirty days," Laurie confided to Leni, "but your visa will probably emerge out of the system before the 90 days expires."

They took the shuttle bus back to the Protea Hotel where they swam in the pool before going their room where they enjoyed a delicious room service meal before making love in the king sized bed.

The next day, they were on another South African Airways aircraft heading for Cape Town.

They stayed at the very pleasant, and very expensive, Victoria and Albert Hotel. They booked for ten days. This allowed them time to find a house to rent. Laurie wanted a place in a secluded location and as far from major cities as possible.

The waterfront area is beautiful but much more expensive than Laurie recalled from when he was there last. They had quite a few meals at the luxurious restaurants in the area. Not that the restaurants within the hotel weren't excellent also and they ate there as well.

They bought a second-hand Toyota Camry and Leni was shocked when, as they were given the car that the manager pointed out a switch discretely hidden under the gear shift boot. The idea was, that if the car was being carjacked it would raise the alarm and give the location of the vehicle so that a rescue team could be dispatched. The manager was very direct when he gave his instructions. "When (not if – Leni noticed) you get carjacked just press this button and get out and run. Don't worry about the car."

Their first drive in their newly acquired car was to Parrow Arms and Ammo on Vortrekker Road. They spent quite some time looking through the range of pistols available, they bought a pair of <u>Browning Hi Power 9MM P</u> pistols. Each was second hand and were remarkably cheap being only 4500 Rand each. Laurie checked the action of each one and they were perfect and showed no sign of wear. They had plenty of other weapons to choose from but Leni had become familiar with the Browning imitation which she had used whilst in Irian Jaya.

The beautiful V&A shopping Centre adjoined the hotel and the couple enjoyed shopping together. Leni found an attractive Travelon anti-theft bag that she liked which not only had room for her feminine necessities but had room for the pistol. The leather handles were steel reinforced which would preclude anybody from cutting them and stealing the bag. It was cleverly designed to be carried over the shoulder in such a way that would make it hard to snatch. Laurie got himself a camera case which was similarly designed for anti-theft. There was room in the case for his pistol and some ammunition but not for a camera.

They went for a drive to Boulders Beach where a colony African penguins live. Laurie never ceased to be delighted by these self-confident little creatures when they would strut ashore and pass disdainfully without the slightest intimidation past the bikini clad women and their partners sunbaking on the sand. They had nests in the vegetation which was further up the beach past the line of sand. Leni was also captivated by the cute little birds and made many movies of them on her phone.

The city has a cable car to Table Mountain which they visited twice. The view is magnificent and there are superb restaurants up there as well. Leni like every other tourist fell in love with the dassie. This is a brown, furry little mammal and which surprisingly is closely related to the elephant.

As a tourist destination, they found that Cape Town had a lot to offer.

Laurie managed to catch up with three of his old pals from the South African Police Service when they all had dinner together. Two of the men were still serving officers but one had retired. They were sad to say that the violence in the country had become much worse since he had left. Lack of resourcing, corruption in the service and the promotion of officers based on their political leaning and not their skill had taken a toll. "Don't get me wrong," one of the men whose name was Brett Erasmus said, "there are many excellent black guys in the service but they are as pissed off as we are with government interference."

It was a happy occasion. There were lots of stories about various other acquaintances some funny and some tragic. Although it was a discussion by four very alpha males they all very courteously included Leni in the discussions and answered the few very superficial questions that she asked. They also listened very intently when she spoke of her experiences during the riots of Glodok Plaza. They asked Laurie why he was in South Africa and he told them his story very accurately and completely.

The two serving officers were both captains and each gave one of their business cards to Laurie as the dinner concluded and the group stood to go their separate ways. "If you ever get bored with your playboy lifestyle, I'm sure that we can reactivate your commission." The second officer whose name was Joe Hepworth remarked with a laugh but the request was clearly genuine. There were man hugs all around and kisses for Leni and they departed.

Chapter 19 – Starting A New Life

The house that Laurie and Leni had decided to rent was in a small coastal village called Strandfontein which was located in the Matzikama Municipality, in the Western Cape province.

They set out early and headed north on the N7. The road was nothing spectacular being just a two-lane highway. What astounded Leni was the behavior of the motorists. The road had a yellow line marked along each side of the road which marked the edge. The line was drawn approximately one metre from the actual edge of the bitumen. Whenever they came up behind a slower moving vehicle, Laurie simply needed to flash his headlights and the driver would pull over and straddle the yellow line to enable their car to pass easily and safely. What was quite astounding was that if an oncoming vehicle was encountered during the passing, that vehicle would also pull over to straddle the yellow line to enable the passing vehicle to do so in safety.

When she discussed the situation with Laurie, he replied that the practice was actually illegal but South African motorists had been doing it for so long that it had become ingrained in the driving culture of the nation.

"In Australia, the government treats drivers like idiots and they behave that way. Here in the RSA, the police are much too busy to be handing out fines and so most drivers learn to drive with common sense and courtesy." Laurie remarked with some conviction in his voice.

As they drove north, they discussed how the AIDS crisis had gripped the country. They passed quite a few informal cemeteries with numerous makeshift crosses signifying the impact that the disease had wrought in small communities.

"These highways that run from the north of Africa to the south have been the artery through which the disease has spread through the country. Drivers have acquired the disease and have spread it as they had liaisons with willing partners up and down the roads." Laurie remarked.

Almost as if to illustrate the point, the Camry came up behind a large semitrailer driving ahead of them. Along with the name and logo of the trucking company the rear doors of the trailer also had painted on them, a large representation of the red bow that was the symbol of the anti AIDS movement. As they got closer the vehicle swung to the left and Leni thought that it was just pulling over to let them pass. But No! It actually pulled completely off the road in a great cloud of dust and stopped. As they passed the stationary vehicle, Leni saw the passenger door of the cabin opening and a young woman who was dressed very provocatively could be seen climbing up into the cabin.

"WTS?" Leni asked, using the commonly used Indonesian acronym for Wanita Tuna Susila which basically refers to a prostitute. They had been lapsing back and forth in English and Bahasa Indonesian as they always did when they were alone together.

"Yep," Leni replied, "sad isn't it. The driver obviously knows about the disease but yet he will stop to pick up a hooker from the side of the road."

They decided to stop at Citrusdal after a drive of about three hours. Lauri had arranged to catch up with a guy named Casper Coetzee who was also one of his former colleagues along with Casper's lovely wife Zelda. He was the local police Captain and they had insisted, by email before they had left Capetown that they would stay two nights with them. They had a delightful barbeque that evening with Casper and Zelda displaying their excellent culinary skills. The following day, Laurie and Casper played a game at the delightful

175

nine-hole golf course. Zelda introduced Leni to the delights of hiking on the Buchu Hiking Trail followed by relaxation in the hot springs that were available in the wonderfully maintained Cape Dutch buildings at the end of the trail.

They departed the following morning with Laurie again being asked, this time by Casper, if he would like to rejoin the force.

They continued to drive north and encountered a gang of youths wandering about on the road at an intersection north of Clanwilliam. Laurie told Leni to get her pistol out and be ready to fire it. He slowed down somewhat but straddled the centerline of the road and blasted the horn. It was evident to the youths that, not only was he not going to stop, but he was not able to stop and that anybody who stood in front of the car would be killed. The gang scattered as the car approached and they sped past.

"They were probably harmless, just wanting to sell souvenirs, but you can't be sure." Laurie remarked.

"Happens in Indonesia too." Leni replied.

"Yes – that's true."

They drove on to the quaint settlement of Klawer which on the "welcome" sign near the start of the town, there was what Leni called a "club" because that is what it looked like.

"Are there other towns called spades diamonds and hearts?" she asked laughing.

"'fraid not," Laurie laughed, "Klawer is the Afrikaans name for the clover that grows like crazy around here at certain times of year.

They drove around the town looking for the address of the landlords of the house that they were planning to rent at Strandfontein. Eventually they found it and were invited inside by a very nice couple who were in their late fifties. Over scones and crème washed down by a delightfully brewed coffee, they discovered that the house that they were going to rent had been owned by the woman's parents. The old couple had moved to a nursing home two years ago, where her father had subsequently died. Her mother, who now suffers from dementia, lives on and she is convinced that she will move back to the house when she gets well again. She has forgotten the death of her husband and believes that he is waiting for her at the house.

The daughter and son in law can't bring themselves to sell the house until after the mother passes away. The son remarked to Laurie, "poor old Stewart was a very good tradesman in his day and the house has a very nice workshop and a boat garaged there. I have left it the way it was when Stewart was alive, but if you want to use the boat, feel free."

So, with sets of house keys in their pocket, along with instructions on how to use the cable TV, the internet router and the boat along with maps showing the best places to fish. Not to mention more scones and crème, Leni and Laurie made their way back to the Camry.

Almost two hours later they were moving into a grand old house overlooking the ocean. It had clearly been a house that had been occupied by an elderly couple. There were rails in the shower and beside the toilet. The boat in the garage was clean and well maintained. The workshop had a shadow board with many tools each hanging in their nominated places. There were shelves with many bottles and boxes of nails and screws of a large variety of shapes and sizes, all carefully laid out in logical order. The various horizontal surfaces in the living room and bedrooms all had crocheted doilies under beautiful old art pieces. There was a photo hanging on the wall of the old couple on their wedding day and recognizable photos of the daughter as a child also hanging in what must have been the room in which she grew up.

Laurie and Leni had bought some groceries from the Spar store in Klawer but after they had settled in and lit the fire, they were tired. They decided to have dinner at the local (and only) seafood restaurant.

They came back after a delightful meal where they had been interrogated by well-meaning locals who wanted to get to know this exotic couple, an Australian and an Indonesian who had suddenly appeared amongst them.

The fire had died back to embers but the house was warm and cozy. They stripped naked and lay on the sheepskin rug in front of a restoked fire and made love in what they had hoped was going to be their new home for years to come.

Chapter 20 – The Past Catches Up

The next morning, Laurie connected his laptop to the Internet via the very slow modem provided and also figured out how to get the cable TV working.

The first email that arrived was from the lawyers acting for PT Copper Co asking if he would be prepared to travel to Jakarta to give evidence in the outstanding case that they had been trying to get to court for many months. They offered to fly him business class to Jakarta and they would pay him his consulting rate of $US2200 per day for the five days that he would be required to be there. The case was due for hearing in three weeks' time.

He discussed this with Leni who did not want him to leave and particularly did not want him going to Indonesia. Despite this, she knew that this appearance would be very helpful to his career but more importantly, she realized that his appearance would strike a blow against the corruption that was destroying the fabric of her country. She also said that because it was her that they really wanted to kill, she felt that if she was not with him then he would be safe.

So, he replied that he would be available and he asked them to book him into the Ascott Hotel on JL Kebon Kachang Raya where he had stayed before. It had good security, excellent rooms and good food. It was cheaper than many other Jakarta hotels like the Grand Indonesia on the other side of the street but that didn't matter because the client would be paying the bill. He asked the company to book a flight for him from Brisbane to Jakarta. He did not tell them that he was in the RSA and had decided to fly from South Africa to Brisbane at his own expense and on his RSA passport.

He received another email:

My vriend,

Be careful.

They are still looking for you but they don't know where you are.

Nor do I - let's keep it that way.

Cheers

Jakob_regop10inch

They decided that they couldn't be much more careful than they were.

A week went by and Laurie had decided to take the boat out because the folks at the restaurant had told him that the fishing was good and the late Stewart had known all the best spots.

He did not have a tow bar on the Camry with which to move the boat and he arranged to have one fitted by a vendor at Klawer. He decided to drop in on his landlords and after more scones and tea, he drove back to Strandfontein. Not only did he now have the means to tow the boat to the sea, he had instructions on where to fish from Dougal, the son in law, who had often gone out with Stewart in happier times.

As he was leaving Klawer, his phone rang. Had it been a few minutes later, he would have missed the call because the mobile phone coverage only covered the towns in the area (albeit unreliably) and not the roads in between.

It was Casper. "Mate," he said. He wasn't in the habit of calling people 'mate' but he did when talking to Laurie in recognition of his being Australian. He continued, speaking in Afrikaans. "I had an Indonesian guy named Mohammad Halim asking one of my officers where you live. He claimed to be Leni's brother in law."

"Leni doesn't have a brother in law."

"Yeah, I figured that. My guy didn't tell him anything and said that he didn't know of any Australians with an Indonesian companion living around here. That was the truth because I am the only one who knows that you are here."

"OK! Many thanks for the heads up. I'd better hang up now and call Leni to tell her to lock the house up tight and keep her gun handy."

"Aren't you with her?"

"No! She's still in Strandfontein, I'm in Klawer buying some stuff."

"OK – call her. Let me know how you get on."

Laurie pressed off the call and then called Leni's phone on speed dial.

"Beee Boop; The number that you have called is out of range. Please leave a message and dial again."

He dialed again.

Same.

He pressed Casper's number from the 'Recents' window. After a couple of tones that indicated ringing, Casper answered.

"Hello"

"Casper, its Laurie again, she is not answering. I'm heading back to Strandfontein."

"OK – Don't do anything foolish."

"I won't – thanks, Goodbye"

"Goodbye"

Laurie accelerated the Camry and weaved past a blue SUV and was glared at by the driver, before speeding back breaking every speed limit on the R362 as he drove the 70km back to their house.

The front door was locked. This was to be expected and he inserted his key and opened the door as he called Leni's name. He heard a sound coming from the living room. It was from a human female voice but he couldn't make out what she said. He hurried to the living room now with his pistol clutched between his hands ready to fire.

The first thing he saw in the room was a big African man, probably a Zulu, holding a pistol and pointing it at him. The other thing that he saw was Leni naked and pinned to the wall with nails through the palms of her outstretched hands. She was standing on a chair and gagged with a piece of cloth torn from the blouse that she had been wearing.

It was an impasse between Laurie and the African. Each pointing the gun at the other. Laurie tried to intimidate him. "Drop the gun he yelled."

The African merely smiled.

Next Laurie felt a cold hard barrel pushed against his skull and a voice, speaking in Bahasa Indonesian, say, "Uncock your gun and put it on the floor. Otherwise I will blow your brains out and kick away the chair that your little Cina slut is standing on."

Laurie did as he had been instructed.

"Are you Halim?" Laurie asked.

"Yes, I am," he replied, "and this is my friend Gazini. His name means blood and he wants to see some."

He instructed Gazini to bring a chair from the adjacent kitchen which was the same as the one that Leni was standing on. He used simple English words without sentences which indicated that the African did not speak English very well.

He made Laurie sit on the chair which he positioned about two metres from the wall and facing Leni.

The woman's face was very flushed and tears were rolling down and dripping off her chin as she wailed into the gag from the fear and the agony of her punctured hands.

Halim said, "Rope!" as he pantomimed with his hands a tying action and pointed towards the workshop. Cazini went to find some.

Minutes later, he returned. He had lengths of orange colored 5mm thick rope which Laurie knew that he must have cut from a crab pot that had been stashed against the wall near the boat.

Hasson pointed to Laurie and Gazini understood and began tying Laurie to the chair. He tied his ankles to the front legs of the chair and then he tied his wrists to a bar that formed the lower section of the back of the chair.

"Now we wait," said Halim.

"What for," asked Laurie.

"Don't be impatient, Mr. Truck, you are wishing your life away. We are waiting for General Setepu. He is very annoyed at you. You killed our two friends Hidayat and Hasan. I don't feel sorry for Hidayat. Trying to shoot the driver of a moving car from a motorcycle was dumb and I don't wonder that you killed him easily. But Hasan had planned his attack carefully and waited until just when you had begun to travel home before trying to sink your boat. They had enjoyed watching your slut here and her harlot friend showing off their bodies on the sand. The General will be very pleased that we have caught you alive. He will delight in seeing you beheaded and we will kick away this chair and leave your slut to hang crucified as she watches the flies swarm over your body."

Laurie struggled to free his hands but to no avail.

"Where is Setepu?" Laurie shouted.

"Don't be impatient, he will be here very soon. They went looking for you and saw you in Klawer. They wanted to drive you off the road but their SUV was not able to catch up with your Camry."

Minutes later, a blue SUV pulled up outside and two Indonesians came into the room. One was a well dresses individual wearing a batik shirt under a suit coat. The other was a giant of a man, with jagged teeth and a battered face. He was shabbily dressed in levis that were dirty and worn.

Leni squirmed when she saw them and tried to speak despite her gag. Only a series of desperate noises were heard.

"Yes! you treacherous little slut," the well-dressed individual remarked, "you remember me from the Defense Centre don't you. Well, no longer will we need to worry about what you might or might not have heard."

Then turning to Laurie, he said, "and you, Sir Galahad, saving your damsel in distress. I am amazed that you were so stupid that you failed to realize that we didn't crash the plane for her but it was for you. Your evidence that you are planning to give next week will shut down many carefully executed schemes that we have arranged to fund our Leader, General Makarim's, run for President. What is worse, is that the evidence itself would be damaging to the general at this critical time."

"So, you had to find us fast!" Laurie asked.

"Yes, and it was difficult. We have many friends in the Australian system but finding Muslims in the South African system who were sympathetic to our cause or who could be intimidated to support it was not easy. Still, as you can see, it was not impossible."

"Shall I kill him now?" asked Halim who was holding a kitchen knife in his hand.

"No!" said Setepu. "We have worked hard for this. Let's enjoy this slut's body before we do anything else. We can leave Sir Galahad alive to see how futile were his efforts to save his little Christian Cina. You did well Mohammad, to nail her hands so that she can die like the false prophet that she believes in. We will kick away the chair after we are finished with her. The last Christian that I did that to took seven days to die."

Setepu lowered his fly and took out his erect penis. "I will take her first and then, you others can have her but be sure to finish with your big black assistant..." he said pointing at Gazini who was unaware of what they were saying since they were speaking in Bahasa Indonesian. Halim stood close behind Setepu and was obviously eager for his turn at the gang rape. The

African had quickly understood what was on offer and smiled in anticipation. The ugly assistant stood back and watched as Setepu stepped up onto the chair and slapped Leni across her face. He was attempting to insert himself into her when his head exploded.

All eyes turned to the ugly Indonesian with a smoking pistol in his hand. Halim had put his gun down but the African was still holding his. His eyes looked at the Indonesian in wonderment as a small red hole appeared beside his wide black nose and the back of his head blew away as a fog of brain and tissue followed it. He was dead before the sound of the gunshot reached his ears.

Halim ran in a futile attempt to escape and the big man aimed his gun at the man's groin and fired. The crotch of his trousers immediately went red and puffed up with the remnants of the testicles and the penis that moments previously was tumescent and ready to rape the defenseless woman before him. He crashed to the floor screaming as he held his groin with blood soaked hands.

The big ugly man dropped the weapon and ran to Leni, He undid her gag. They saw that not only had she been gagged with the cloth from her blouse but that they had forced her panties into her mouth first. She coughed and gasped for air before squealing, "Ujang, Ujang how did you get here?"

The big man stroked her face gently and said nothing as he wiped the bits of Setepu's blood and brain from her face. He turned to Laurie and picked up the kitchen knife and cut the ropes binding his wrists. When his hands were free, he handed Laurie the knife and watched for the few seconds needed for him to cut his ankles free.

The two men, both strangers to each other, then turned to the sobbing naked crucified woman that they both cared about so very much.

Ujang took hold of the head a nail and tried to pull it out. He was about to try to wriggle it when Laurie rested his hand on the big man's tensed grip and said, "stop!"

"If you wriggle the nail, not only will it hurt her terribly but it will likely damage her hand even more. Wait a minute."

He dashed away.

He soon returned with a couple of 32 teeth per inch hacksaw blades from the workshop. Ujang immediately understood what he had in mind and took one blade and slid it between the back of the woman's hand and the wall and began carefully cutting the nail. Laurie did the same with her other hand.

Soon she was free and they lifted her down from the chair and gently sat her down on the setee.

Laurie rang the South African emergency number,10111, and requested that police and ambulance units be dispatched to their address urgently. The operator very professionally advised that she had arranged for that to happen right away. Then she told him to stay calm and asked if she could give any medical advice.

Laurie said, "no" and then "goodbye" before he pressed off the call.

Barely a minute later, the operator called back to tell him that a police car had been dispatched from Lutzville thirty minutes previously, and will be there very soon.

Sobbing and in great pain from her still penetrated hands Leni asked Ujang how he came to be there.

He explained that Hendrik had been contacted by "some guy from Freeport named Johann who said that he had heard that Setepu was looking for you". Hendrik spoke to General Makarim and claimed that he also wanted to kill you to salvage his family's honor. He offered my services. "It has been hard to hang out with them especially when they beat up the wife of a Muslim government official in Johannesburg to make him find out where you were."

During this time, Halim was writhing on the floor, howling in agony, and desperately trying to stem the flow of blood from his groin. The trio on the couch ignored him.

The police car from Lutzville arrived soon after and one officer produced a pair of flat splints from the car's first aid kit and carefully bound Leni's hands to them. They prevented her from flexing her hand which was probably a good thing to do. The other officer tried ineffectually to stem the flow of blood from Halim's groin. The Indonesian thug was moaning softly as he became progressively weaker from blood loss.

The officers examined the bodies of the other two men and collected papers from their pockets. They examined Halim's papers as well.

In the hour that it took for the ambulance to arrive, they took statements from Leni, Laurie and Ujang. Ujang pretended that his English was so bad that he required Laurie to translate. This ensured that they gave a consistent story to the officers. Not that they had anything to be ashamed of but in a case involving two homicides and a critical injury to a third, not to mention the injury to Leni's hands, Laurie knew the importance of being careful and concise in the answers that he gave.

By the time that the ambulance arrived, the situation had escalated to three homicides as Halim had died. Very soon after the arrival of the ambulance, Casper and a very intelligent young black female officer arrived also. Casper took Laurie aside to discussed what had happened.

"Leave this to us." Casper instructed. The ambulance took Leni to the nearest hospital which was in Vredendal. and Laurie went with her sitting beside her

while he stroked her face and carefully pulled parts of
Setepu's brain out of her hair.

Chapter 21 - Epilog

Leni was admitted to the hospital and the doctors and nurses treated her wonderfully well. She was given a local anesthetic and they carefully removed the nails from her palms. They minimized the risk of causing further damage by filing the edges of the nails smooth where they had been hacksawed through and then gently pulled them through her hand.

Laurie stayed overnight with her in the hospital and the staff appreciated it since with both hands splinted and bandaged, she was totally helpless.

Ujang arrived the next day in the Camry. He had packed a couple of suitcases and he and Laurie drove in shifts all the way to Cape town.

She went to see a microsurgeon at the Groote Schuur Hospital. It is the same place where decades previously, Dr Christian Barnard had performed the first heart transplant.

Fortunately, the skillful doctor was able to fix almost all of the damage to Leni's hands although she did finish up with a numbness in the index finger of her left hand. She could have had one hand done at a time but she decided to have both done together so that she could resume her life as soon as possible.

Leni spent two months in Cape Town while she recuperated. Ujang drove back to Strandfontein and arranged tradesmen to fix the fix the wall that Leni had been nailed to. This required a major rebuild since the animals had bashed in the plasterboard in order to located the vertical pine studs into which they drove in the nails. He also got the floor repaired where they had broken into the house from underneath. The landlord offered to get it paid for by insurance but Laurie didn't want him to be inconvenienced in the slightest way.

The very favorable exchange rate made quality medical care much less expensive than was the case in other countries, especially Australia. Laurie used this as an excuse to offer to pay for orthodontic work for Ujang. He would have done it anyway for this loyal and brave man. But, he refused. The man who could boldly face down armed terrorists was afraid of a dentist.

After two months, when there was nothing further for Ujang to do, he flew back to Jakarta.

Laurie travelled to Indonesia as planned and gave his evidence which, as expected, not only ruined the prospects of General Makarim's run for the presidency but left him fighting to avoid a term in prison.

President Habibie was dumped as president and a desperate MPR choose a blind incompetent Muslim cleric named Abdurrahman Wahid as the new president. His shambolic term in office lasted barely one year before he was replaced by Megawati Sukarno Putri. This brought the era of religious dominated presidential elections in Indonesia to an end and Megawati performed reasonably well as the first secularly elected president.

Had Makarim seized power the history of the great nation of Indonesia would have turned out much differently.

Laurie got an email from Johann:

My vriend,

Leni might be interested to know that her 'pal' Rudi Ryadi the former manager from the Defense Headquarters has been found severely bashed in an alley near Pasa Raya.

Nobody knows who did it.

Ujang will be working with me at Freeport for a while.

Cheers

Jakob_regop10inch

Leni suffered a bout of severe depression that lasted for around six months after her frightening and painful experience. The psychological counseling in

South Africa for people suffering Post Traumatic Stress Disorder is world class because sadly that service is in considerable demand in that violent country. Laurie arranged the very best treatment for her.

He also had his own ideas on how to cheer her up. He would take her fishing in the late Stewart's boat and they enjoyed many trips around the beautiful country. They had a particularly romantic trip to the Victoria falls in Zambia. This was followed one month later when he took her for three beautiful weeks to the Sun City Resort and its adjacent animal parks.

They went back to Australia to live at Caloundra much to the disappointment of the friends that they had made in South Africa. Laurie took her riding again on the Harley which had been immaculately cared for by Brian.

Hendrick was very successful in securing a senior position in the new administration and Joyce and little Amber came to visit Leni and Laurie in Caloundra.

The three beautiful women of Chinese descent, Leni, Joyce and Wendy enjoyed going to restaurants, shopping centers and the Caloundra RSL (Returned Serviceman's League) where the locals assumed them to be sisters. Amber, now a toddler and quite a little chatterbox, reveled in the attention that she received from her two 'aunties'.

The house became rather crowded when Leni's mother, Gladys, also arrived from Jakarta. The old lady was every bit the colorful character that Leni and Joyce had described her to be and amongst the humor and the chaos that she brought, Leni did eventually manage to put the ghastly events that had dogged her life for the past year behind her. The episodes of dark misery and suicidal thoughts ceased to be frequent and became progressively more rare. Her demeanor gradually returned to that of her previous cheerful and sexually voracious self.

It gladdened her greatly when they received an email from Naomi to say that she would be travelling to Jakarta next month to begin her degree in Medicine. She expressed her heartfelt gratitude to "Truck" for making it possible for her. They had all agreed to meet back at her family's house in Tana Toraja in twelve months' time when Naomi would be on her first semester break.

More than anything else, the one event that made her outlook on life become positively exuberant was when she felt the first kicks of a tiny little future Australian citizen who had begun taking shape in her womb.

THE END

www.ingramcontent.com/pod-product-compliance
Lightning Source LLC
Chambersburg PA
CBHW072134170626
46813CB00004BA/1561